Let's Enjoy Maste

The Little Prince
小王子

Original Author Antoine de Saint-Exupery
Illustrator Antoine de Saint-Exupery

WORDS
800

MP3

Let's Enjoy Masterpieces!

All the beautiful fairy tales and masterpieces that you have encountered during your childhood remain as warm memories in your adulthood. This time, let's indulge in the world of masterpieces through English. You can enjoy the depth and beauty of original works, which you can't enjoy through Chinese translations.

The stories are easy for you to understand because of your familiarity with them. When you enjoy reading, your ability to understand English will also rapidly improve.

This series of ***Let's Enjoy Masterpieces*** is a special reading comprehension booster program, devised to improve reading comprehension for beginners whose command of English is not satisfactory, or who are elementary, middle, and high school students. With this program, you can enjoy reading masterpieces in English with fun and efficiency.

This carefully planned program is composed of 5 levels, from the beginner level of 350 words to the intermediate and advanced levels of 1,000 words. With this program's level-by-level system, you are able to read famous texts in English and to savor the true pleasure of the world's language.

The program is well conceived, composed of reader-friendly explanations of vocabulary to help the student learn vocabulary and understand the meaning of the texts, and fabulous illustrations that adorn every page.

In addition, with our "Guide to Listening," not only is reading comprehension enhanced but also listening comprehension skills are highlighted.

In the audio recording of the book, texts are vividly read by professional American voice actors. The texts are rewritten, according to the levels of the readers by an expert editorial staff of native speakers, on the basis of standard American English with the ministry of education recommended vocabulary. Therefore, it will be of great help even for all the students that want to learn English.

Please indulge yourself in the fun of reading and listening to English through Let's Enjoy Masterpieces.

How to Use This Book

本書使用說明

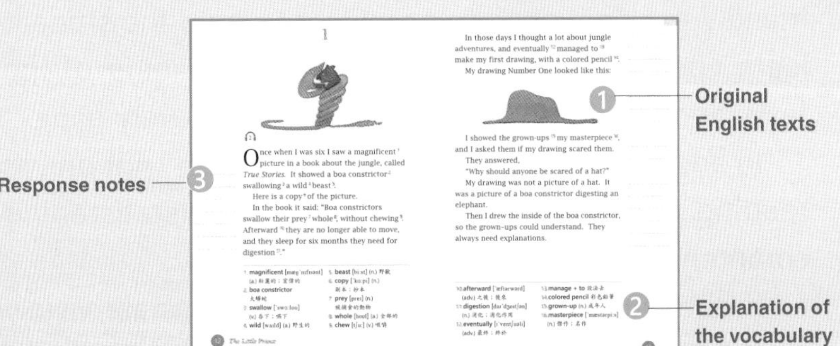
1

Once when I was six I saw a magnificent[1] picture in a book about the jungle, called *True Stories*. It showed a boa constrictor[2] swallowing[3] a wild[4] beast[5].

Here is a copy[6] of the picture.

In the book it said: "Boa constrictors swallow their prey[7] whole[8], without chewing[9]. Afterward[10] they are no longer able to move, and they sleep for six months they need for digestion[11]."

In those days I thought a lot about jungle adventures, and eventually[12] managed to[13] make my first drawing, with a colored pencil[14].

My drawing Number One looked like this:

I showed the grown-ups[15] my masterpiece[16], and I asked them if my drawing scared them.

They answered,

"Why should anyone be scared of a hat?"

My drawing was not a picture of a hat. It was a picture of a boa constrictor digesting an elephant.

Then I drew the inside of the boa constrictor, so the grown-ups could understand. They always need explanations.

1 *Original English texts*

It is easy to understand the meaning of the text, because the text is rewritten according to the levels of the readers.

2 *Explanation of the vocabulary*

The words and expressions that include vocabulary above the elementary level are clearly defined.

3 *Response notes*

Spaces are included in the book so you can take notes about what you don't understand or what you want to remember.

Audio Recording

In the audio recording, native speakers narrate the texts in standard American English. By combining the written words and the audio recording, you can listen to English with great ease.

Audio books have been popular in Britain and America for many decades. They allow the listener to experience the proper word pronunciation and sentence intonation that add important meaning and drama to spoken English. Students will benefit from listening to the recording twenty or more times.

After you are familiar with the text and recording, listen once more with your eyes closed to check your listening comprehension. Finally, after you can listen with your eyes closed and understand every word and every sentence, you are then ready to mimic the native speaker.

Then you should make a recording by reading the text yourself. Then play both recordings to compare your oral skills with those of a native speaker.

CONTENTS

Introduction

安托萬・德・聖艾修伯里

Antoine de Saint-Exupery
(1900–1944)

Born into a family with an aristocratic lineage, Antoine de Saint-Exupery enjoyed a happy childhood. In 1921, Saint-Exupery joined the French air force and became a pilot. After his military service, while looking around for a job, he wrote for magazines. Then, in an attempt to escape from an ordinary life in 1926, Saint-Exupery began to fly for the first airline mail service. These flying experiences provided the basis for *Southern Mail* and *Night Flight*. *Night Flight* won the Prix Femina, and met with acclaim from contemporary writers.

Saint-Exupery's works reflect the process of discovering the meaning of life we are born to live, in the fight against all odds and hardships. When World War II broke out, he flew surveillance missions, and after the German occupation of France, he was exiled to the United States, where he wrote *The Little Prince*.

In 1942, Saint-Exupery reenlisted in the military to fight for the Allies. He took off the night of July 31, 1944 to collect data on German troop movements in the Rhone River Valley, and was never seen again. *The Little Prince* and many of his other well-loved works have been translated into many languages and become classics.

Written in 1943 by Antoine de Saint-Exupery during his exile to the United States, *The Little Prince* is a fairy tale for adults, offering everyone a touch of fantasy and poetry. Saint-Exupery took much from his own life experience as a pilot, including crash landings in the Sahara Desert.

The narrator of the story, a pilot like the author, finds himself stranded in the middle of a desert and meets a little prince from an asteroid. Frustrated with a beautiful but grumpy rose, the prince sets off on a journey. After a long journey, he arrives on Earth and meets a fox. Then, the fox teaches him that it is only with the heart that one can see properly what is essential. *The little prince* learns how important aspects of life are often invisible to the eye, and he has come to understand the true value of the rose.

In the portrayal of characters that the little Prince meets on his travels, the author describes the preciousness of life that adults can't see and tend to forget, as they get older. *The Little Prince* reflects Saint-Exupery's thesis that the true meaning of life can be found in the links that we make with others. The author's beautiful illustrations give the story a poetic and warmly humanistic tone.

TO LEON WERTH

I ask the indulgence of the children who may read this book for dedicating it to a grown-up. I have a serious reason: he is the best friend I have in the world. I have another reason: this grown-up understands everything, even books about children. I have a third reason: he lives in France where he is hungry and cold. He needs cheering up. If all these reasons are not enough, I will dedicate the book to the child from whom this grown-up grew. All grown-ups were once children — although few of them remember it. And so I correct my dedication:

TO LEON WERTH
WHEN HE WAS A LITTLE BOY

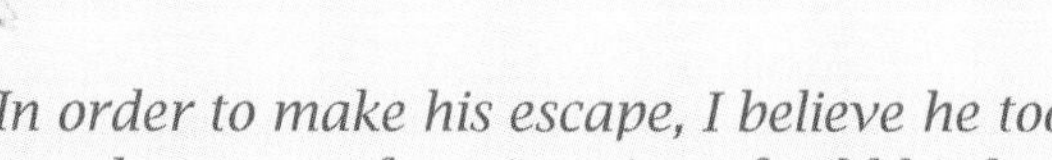

In order to make his escape, I believe he took advantage of a migration of wild birds.

1

2

Once when I was six I saw a magnificent[1] picture in a book about the jungle, called *True Stories*. It showed a boa constrictor[2] swallowing[3] a wild[4] beast[5].

Here is a copy[6] of the picture.

In the book it said: "Boa constrictors swallow their prey[7] whole[8], without chewing[9]. Afterward[10] they are no longer able to move, and they sleep for six months they need for digestion[11]."

---

1. **magnificent** [mæg`nɪfɪsənt] (a.) 壯麗的；宏偉的
2. **boa constrictor** 大蟒蛇
3. **swallow** [`swɑ:lou] (v.) 吞下；嚥下
4. **wild** [waɪld] (a.) 野生的
5. **beast** [bi:st] (n.) 野獸
6. **copy** [`kɑ:pi] (n.) 副本；抄本
7. **prey** [preɪ] (n.) 被捕食的動物
8. **whole** [houl] (a.) 全部的
9. **chew** [tʃu:] (v.) 咀嚼

In those days I thought a lot about jungle adventures, and eventually[12] managed to[13] make my first drawing, with a colored pencil[14].

My drawing *Number One* looked like this:

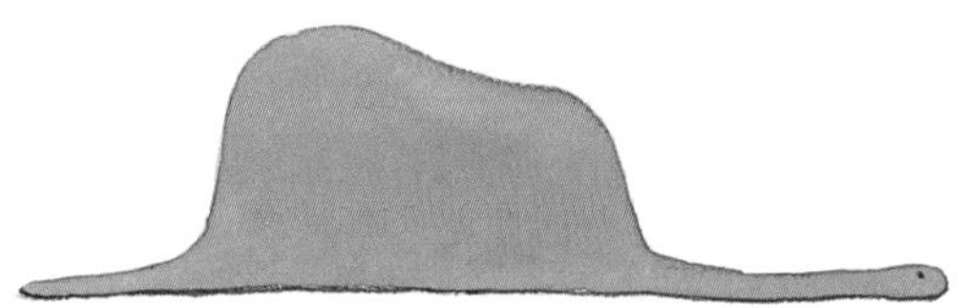

I showed the grown-ups[15] my masterpiece[16], and I asked them if my drawing scared them.

They answered,

"Why should anyone be scared of a hat?"

My drawing was not a picture of a hat. It was a picture of a boa constrictor digesting an elephant.

Then I drew the inside of the boa constrictor, so the grown-ups could understand. They always need explanations.

---

10. **afterward** [`æftərwərd] (adv.) 之後；後來
11. **digestion** [daɪ`dʒestʃən] (n.) 消化；消化作用
12. **eventually** [ɪ`ventʃuəli] (adv.) 最終；終於
13. **manage + to** 設法去
14. **colored pencil** 彩色鉛筆
15. **grown-up** (n.) 成年人
16. **masterpiece** [`mæstərpi:s] (n.) 傑作；名作

My drawing *Number Two* looked like this:

The grown-ups advised me to put away[1] my drawings of boa constrictors, outside or inside, and apply myself instead to[2] geography[3], history, arithmetic[4], and grammar. That is why I gave up[5], at the age of six, a magnificent career as an artist. I had been discouraged[6] by the failure of my drawing *Number One* and of my drawing *Number Two.*

---

1. **put away** 拋棄；收起來
2. **apply oneself to** 請求自己去
3. **geography** [dʒi`ɑ:grəfi] (n.) 地理學
4. **arithmetic** [ə`rɪθmətɪk] (n.) 算術
5. **give up** 放棄
6. **discourage** [dɪs`kɜ:rɪdʒ] (v.) 使洩氣；使沮喪
7. **by oneself** 單獨地
8. **exhausting** [ɪg`zɑ:stɪŋ] (a.) 使人精疲力竭的
9. **career** [kə`rɪr] (n.)（終身）職業

Grown-ups never understand anything by themselves[7], and it is exhausting[8] for children to have to explain over and over again.

So then I had to choose another career[9].

I learned to pilot[10] airplanes. I have flown[11] almost everywhere in the world. And, as a matter of fact[12], geography has been a big help to me. I could tell China from Arizona at first glance[13], which is very useful if you get lost[14] during the night.

So I have met, in the course[15] of my life, lots of serious people. I have spent lots of time with grown-ups. I have seen them at close range[16]. . . which hasn't improved[17] my opinion[18] of them.

---

10. **pilot** [ˋpaɪlət] (v.) 駕駛
11. **fly** [flaɪ] (v.) 飛翔 (fly-flew-flown)
12. **as a matter of fact** 事實上
13. **at a glance** 一瞥
14. **get lost** 迷失方向
15. **course** [kɔ:rs] (n.) 路線；方向
16. **range** [reɪndʒ] (n.) 距離
17. **improve** [ɪmˋpru:v] (v.) 改進；改善
18. **opinion** [əˋpɪnjən] (n.) 意見；見解

Whenever I encountered[1] a grown-up who seemed to be intelligent[2], I would experiment[3] on him with my drawing *Number One*, which I have always kept. I wanted to see if he really understood anything.

But he would always answer, "That's a hat."

Then I wouldn't talk about boa constrictors or jungles or stars. I would put myself on his level and talk about bridge[4] and golf and politics and neckties. And my grown-up was glad to know such a reasonable[5] person.

---

1. **encounter** [ɪn`kaʊntər] (v.) 偶遇
2. **intelligent** [ɪn`telɪdʒənt] (a.) 有才智的
3. **experiment** [ɪk`sperɪmənt] (v.) 進行實驗
4. **bridge** [brɪdʒ] (n.) 橋牌
5. **reasonable** [`ri:zənəbəl] (a.) 通情達理的
6. **crash** [kræʃ] (n.) 墜毀
7. **landing** [`lændɪŋ] (n.) 降落
8. **crash landing** (n.) 迫降
9. **the Sahara Desert** 撒哈拉沙漠
10. **neither** [`ni:ðər] (conj.) 兩者都不
11. **mechanic** [mɪ`kænɪk] (n.) 機械工
12. **passenger** [`pæsəndʒər] (n.) 乘客

2

So I lived all alone, without anyone I could really talk to, until I had to make a crash[6] landing[7,8] in the Sahara Desert[9] six years ago. Something in my plane's engine had broken. Since I had neither[10] a mechanic[11] nor passengers[12] in the plane with me, I was preparing to undertake[13] the difficult repair[14] job by myself. For me it was a matter of life or death: I had only enough drinking water for eight days.

The first night, then, I went to sleep on the sand a thousand miles from any inhabited[15] country. I was more isolated[16] than a man shipwrecked[17] on a raft[18] in the middle of the ocean. So you can imagine my surprise when I was awakened[19] at daybreak[20] by a funny little voice saying, "Please . . . draw me a sheep . . ."

---

13. **undertake** [ˌʌndɚ`teɪk] (v.) 試圖；著手
14. **repair** [rɪ`per] (v.) 修理；修補
15. **inhabited** [ɪn`hæbɪtɪd] (a.) 有居民的
16. **isolated** [`aɪsəleɪtɪd] (a.) 孤立的
17. **shipwreck** [`ʃɪprek] (v.) 船舶失事
18. **raft** [ræft] (n.) 木筏
19. **awaken** [ə`weɪkən] (v.) 喚醒
20. **daybreak** [`deɪbreɪk] (n.) 黎明；破曉

"What?"

"Draw me a sheep . . ."

I leaped up[1] as if I had been struck[2] by lightning[3]. I rubbed[4] my eyes hard. I stared. And I saw an extraordinary[5] little fellow[6] staring back at me very seriously. Here is the best portrait[7] I managed to make of him, later on.

Here is the best portrait I managed to make of him, later on.

But of course my drawing is much less attractive[8] than my model. This is not my fault. My career as a painter was discouraged at the age of six by the grown-ups, and I had never learned to draw anything except boa constrictors, outside and inside.

So I stared wide-eyed[9] at this apparition[10].

Don't forget that I was a thousand miles from any inhabited territory[11]. Yet this little fellow seemed to be neither lost nor dying of exhaustion[12], hunger, or thirst[13]; nor did he seem scared to death[14]. There was nothing in his appearance that suggested a child lost in the middle of the desert a thousand miles from any inhabited territory.

---

1. **leap up** 跳起來
2. **strike** [straɪk] (v.) 打擊；攻擊
3. **lightning** [`laɪtnɪŋ] (n.) 閃電
4. **rub** [rʌb] (v.) 摩擦
5. **extraordinary** [ɪk`strɔ:rdəneri] (a.) 異常的
6. **fellow** [`feloʊ] (n.) 夥伴；人
7. **portrait** [`pɔ:rtrɪt] (n.) 肖像
8. **attractive** [ə`træktɪv] (a.) 有吸引力的
9. **wide-eyed** (a.) 睜大眼的
10. **apparition** [ˌæpər`ɪʃən] (n.) 幽靈；特異景象
11. **territory** [`terɪtɔ:ri] (n.) 領地
12. **exhaustion** [ɪg`zɑ:stʃən] (n.) 枯竭；耗盡
13. **thirst** [θɜ:rst] (n.) 口渴
14. **to death** 極度

When I finally managed to speak, I asked him, "But. . . what are you doing here?"

And then he repeated[1], very slowly and very seriously, "Please . . . draw me a sheep . . ."

When you encounter an overpowering[2] mystery, you don't dare[3] disobey[4]. Absurd[5] as it seemed, a thousand miles from all inhabited regions[6] and in danger of[7] death, I took a piece of paper and a pen out of my pocket. But then I remembered that I had mostly[8] studied geography, history, arithmetic, and grammar, and I told the little fellow (rather crossly[9]) that I didn't know how to draw.

He replied, "That doesn't matter[10.11]. Draw me a sheep."

---

1. **repeat** [rɪ`pi:t] (v.) 重複
2. **overpowering** [ˏouvər`pauərɪŋ] (a.) 不可抗拒的
3. **dare** [der] (v.) 敢
4. **disobey** [ˏdɪsə`beɪ] (v.) 不服從
5. **absurd** [əb`sɜ:rd] (a.) 荒謬的
6. **region** [`ri:dʒən] (n.) 地區
7. **in danger of** 處於……危險之中
8. **mostly** [`moustli] (adv.) 大多數地

Since I had never drawn a sheep, I made him one of the only two drawings I knew how to make—the one of the boa constrictor from outside. And I was astounded[12] to hear the little fellow answer:

"No! No! I don't want an elephant inside a boa constrictor. A boa constrictor is very dangerous, and an elephant would get in the way[13]. Where I live, everything is very small. I need a sheep. Draw me a sheep."

So then I made a drawing.

He looked at it carefully, and then said, "No. This one is already quite sick. Make another."

---

9. **crossly** [ˋkrɑ:sli] (adv.) 相反地
10. **matter** [ˋmætər] (v.) 有關係
11. **That doesn't matter.** 那無所謂。
12. **astounded** [əˋstaʊndɪd] (a.) 被震驚的
13. **get in the way** 妨礙

7

I made another drawing. My friend gave me a kind, indulgent[1] smile:

"You can see for yourself[2]. . . that's not a sheep, it's a ram[3]. It has horns[4]. . ."

So I made my third drawing, but it was rejected[5], like the others:

"This one's too old. I want a sheep that will live a long time."

So then, impatiently[6], since I was in a hurry to start work on my engine, I scribbled[7] this drawing, and added[8], "This is just the crate[9]. The sheep you want is inside."

But I was amazed[10] to see my young critic's[11] face light up[12].

"That's just the kind I wanted! Do you think this sheep will need a lot of grass[13]?"

"Why?"

"Because where I live, everything is very small. . ."

"There's sure to be enough. I've given you a very small sheep."

He bent over[14] the drawing. "Not so small as all that . . . Look! He's gone to sleep . . ."

And that's how I made the acquaintance[15] of the little prince.

---

1. **indulgent** [ɪn`dʌldʒənt] (a.) 溺愛的；寬容的
2. **for oneself** 為自己
3. **ram** [ræm] (n.) 公羊
4. **horn** [hɔːrn] (n.) 角
5. **reject** [rɪ`dʒekt] (v.) 拒絕
6. **impatiently** [ɪm`peɪʃəntli] (adv.) 不耐煩地；急地
7. **scribble** [`skrɪbl] (v.) 潦草地書寫
8. **add** [æd] (v.) 增加
9. **crate** [kreɪt] (n.) 條板箱
10. **amazed** [ə`meɪzd] (a.) 吃驚的
11. **critic** [`krɪtɪk] (n.) 吹毛求疵的人；批評家
12. **light up** 點燃；照亮
13. **grass** [græs] (n.) 青草；牧草
14. **bend over** 折彎過去 (bend-bent-bent)
15. **acquaintance** [ə`kweɪntəns] (n.) 相識；了解 (make the acquaintance of: 與……相識)

3

It took me a long time to understand where he came from[1]. The little prince, who asked me so many questions, never seemed to hear the ones I asked him.

It was things he said quite at random[2] that, bit by bit[3], explained everything. For instance[4], when he first caught sight of[5] my airplane (I won't draw my airplane; that would be much too complicated[6] for me) he asked:

"What's that thing over there?"

"It's not a thing. It flies. It's an airplane. My airplane."

---

1. **come from** 來自
2. **at random** 隨便地；任意地
3. **bit by bit** 漸漸地 (=by bits)
4. **for instance** 例如
5. **catch sight of** 看到
6. **complicated** [`kɑ:mplɪkeɪtɪd] (a.) 複雜的
7. **exclaim** [ɪk`skleɪm] (v.) (由於興奮) 驚呼；驚叫
8. **modestly** [`mɑ:dɪstli] (adv.) 謙虛地；審慎地
9. **break into** 突然開始大笑
10. **peal** [pi:l] (n.) 宏亮而持續的響聲
11. **annoy** [ə`nɔɪ] (v.) 惹惱；使生氣
12. **a good deal** 非常
13. **misfortune** [mɪs`fɔ:rtʃən] (n.) 不幸；厄運
14. **planet** [`plænɪt] (n.) 行星

And I was proud to tell him I could fly.

Then he exclaimed[7]:

"What! You fell out of the sky?"

"Yes," I said modestly[8].

"Oh! That's funny . . ." And the little prince broke into[9] a lovely peal[10] of laughter, which annoyed[11] me a good deal[12]. I like my misfortunes[13] to be taken seriously. Then he added, "So you fell out of the sky, too. What planet[14] are you from?"

9

That was when I had the first clue[1] to the mystery of his presence[2], and I questioned him sharply.

"Do you come from another planet?"

But he made no answer. He shook his head[3] a little, still staring at my airplane.

"Of course, *that* couldn't have brought you from very far. . ."

And he fell into a reverie[4] that lasted a long while. Then, taking my sheep out of his pocket, he plunged into[5] contemplation[6] of his treasure[7].

You can imagine how intrigued[8] I was by this hint[9] about "other planets." I tried to learn more: "Where do you come from, little fellow? Where is this 'where I live' of yours? Where will you be taking my sheep?"

After a thoughtful[10] silence he answered, "The good thing about the crate you've given me is that he can use it for a house after dark."

---

1. **clue** [klu:] (n.) 線索；跡象
2. **presence** [ˋprezəns] (n.) 存在
3. **shake one's head** 搖頭
4. **reverie** [ˋrevəri] (n.) 白日夢；幻想
5. **plunge into** 跳入；投入
6. **contemplation** (n.) 沉思
7. **treasure** [ˋtreʒər] (n.) 寶藏

"Of course. And if you're good, I'll give you a rope to tie him up[11] during the day. And a stake[12] to tie him to."

This proposition[13] seemed to shock the little prince.

"Tie him up? What a funny idea!"

"But if you don't tie him up, he'll wander off[14] somewhere and get lost."

My friend burst out[15] laughing again.

"Where could he go?"

"Anywhere. Straight ahead . . ."

Then the little prince remarked[16] quite seriously, "Even if he did, everything's so small where I live!" And he added, perhaps a little sadly, "Straight ahead, you can't go very far."

8. **intrigue** [ɪn`tri:g] (v.) 激起……的好奇心
9. **hint** [hɪnt] (n.) 暗示
10. **thoughtful** [`θɑ:tfəl] (a.) 深思的；沉思的
11. **tie up** 繫住
12. **stake** [steɪk] (n.) 樁；棍子
13. **proposition** [ˌprɑ:pə`zɪʃən] (n.) 建議；提議
14. **wander off** 到……閒逛
15. **burst out + V-ing** 突然……起來
16. **remark** [rɪ`mɑ:rk] (v.) 談到；說

10

4

That was how I had learned a second very important thing, which was that the planet he came from was hardly[1] bigger than a house!

That couldn't surprise me much. I knew very well that except for the huge planets like Earth, Jupiter[2], Mars[3], and Venus[4], which have been given names, there are hundreds of others that are sometimes so small that it's very difficult to see them through a telescope[5]. When an astronomer[6] discovers one of them, he gives it a number instead of a name. For instance, he would call it "Asteroid[7] 325."

I have serious[8] reasons to believe that the planet the little prince came from is Asteroid B-612.

---

1. **hardly** [`hɑ:rdli] (adv.) 幾乎不；簡直不
2. **Jupiter** [`dʒu:pɪtər] (n.) 木星
3. **Mars** [mɑ:rz] (n.) 火星
4. **Venus** [`vi:nəs] (n.) 金星
5. **telescope** [`teləskoup] (n.) 望遠鏡
6. **astronomer** [ə`strɑ:nəmər] (n.) 天文學家 (astronaut: 太空人)
7. **asteroid** [`æstərɔɪd] (n.) 小行星
8. **serious** [`sɪriəs] (a.) 認真的
9. **sight** [saɪt] (v.) 看見；發現

This asteroid has been sighted[9] only once by telescope, in 1909 by a Turkish[10] astronomer, who had then made a formal[11] demonstration[12] of his discovery at an International Astronomical[13] Congress[14]. But no one had believed him on account of[15] the way he was dressed. Grown-ups are like that.

10. **Turkish** [ˋtɜ:rkɪʃ] (a.) 土耳其的

11. **formal** [ˋfɔ:rməl] (a.) 正式的

12. **demonstration** [ˏdemənˋstreɪʃən] (n.) 證明；論證

13. **astronomical** [ˏæstrəˋnɑ:mɪkəl] (a.) 天文學的

14. **congress** [ˋkɑ:ŋgrɪs] (n.) (正式)會議；代表大會

15. **on account of** 因為；由於

11

Fortunately for the reputation[1] of Asteroid B-612, a Turkish dictator[2] ordered his people, on pain of[3] death, to wear European clothes. The astronomer repeated his demonstration in 1920, wearing a very elegant[4] suit[5]. And this time everyone believed him.

---

1. **reputation** [ˌrepjuˋteɪʃən] (n.) 名譽；名聲
2. **dictator** [ˋdɪkteɪtər] (n.) 獨裁者
3. **on pain of death** 以死論處
4. **elegant** [ˋelɪgənt] (a.) 優雅的
5. **suit** [su:t] (n.) 衣服；套裝
6. **detail** [diˋteɪl] (n.) 細節；詳情

If I've told you these details[6] about Asteroid B-612 and if I've given you its number, it is on account of the grown-ups. Grown-ups like numbers. When you tell them about a new friend, they never ask questions about what really matters[7].

They never ask: "What does his voice sound like?" "What games does he like best?" "Does he collect butterflies?"

They ask: "How old is he?" "How many brothers does he have?" "How much does he weigh[8]?" "How much money does his father make?"

Only then do they think they know him. If you tell grown-ups, "I saw a beautiful red brick[9] house, with geraniums[10] at the windows and doves[11] on the roof . . . ," they won't be able to imagine such a house. You have to tell them, "I saw a house worth[12] a hundred thousand francs[13]." Then they exclaim, "What a pretty house!"

---

7. **matter** [ˋmætər] (v.) 有關係；要緊
8. **weigh** [weɪ] (v.) 有……重量
9. **brick** [brɪk] (a.) 磚砌的
10. **geranium** [dʒəˋreɪniəm] (n.) 天竺葵
11. **dove** [dʌv] (n.) 鴿子
12. **worth** [wɜːrθ] (a.) 值……錢的
13. **franc** [fræŋk] (n.) 法郎

12

So if you tell them: "The proof[1] of the little prince's existence[2] is that he was delightful[3], that he laughed, and that he wanted a sheep. When someone wants a sheep, that proves he exists," they shrug[4] their shoulders and treat[5] you like a child!

But if you tell them: "The planet he came from is Asteroid B-612," then they'll be convinced[6], and they won't bother[7] you with their questions. That's the way they are. You must not hold it against[8] them. Children should be very understanding[9] of grown-ups.

But, of course, those of us who understand life couldn't care[10] less about numbers! I should have liked to begin this story like a fairy tale[11]. I should have liked to say:

1. **proof** [pru:f] (n.) 證據
2. **existence** [ɪg`zɪstəns] (n.) 存在
3. **delightful** [dɪ`laɪtfəl] (a.) 令人愉快的
4. **shrug** [ʃrʌg] (v.) 聳肩
5. **treat** [tri:t] (v.) 對待
6. **convinced** [kən`vɪnst] (a.) 確信的
7. **bother** [`bɑ:ðər] (v.) 打擾
8. **hold against** 歸咎於……
9. **understanding** [ˏʌndər`stændɪŋ] (a.) 理解他人的
10. **care** [ker] (v.) 關心；在乎
11. **fairy tale** 童話故事
12. **once upon a time** 從前

"Once upon a time[12] there was a little prince who lived on a planet hardly any bigger than he was, and who needed a friend . . ." For those who understand life, that would sound[13] much truer.

The fact is, I don't want my book to be taken lightly. Telling these memories is so painful[14] for me. It's already been six years since my friend went away, taking his sheep with him.

If I try to describe[15] him here, it's so I won't forget him. It's sad to forget a friend. Not everyone has had a friend. And I might become like the grown-ups who are no longer interested in anything but numbers. Which is still another reason why I've bought a box of paints[16] and some pencils. It's hard to go back to drawing, at my age, when you've never made any attempts[17] since the one of a boa from inside and the one of a boa from outside, at the age of six!

---

13. **sound** [saʊnd] (v.)
聽起來；感覺
14. **painful** [ˋpeɪnfəl]
(a.) 令人痛苦的
15. **describe** [dɪˋskraɪb]
(v.) 描述；描繪
16. **paint** [peɪnt] (n.)
繪畫顏料；塗料
17. **attempt** [əˋtempt]
(n.) 企圖；嘗試

13

I'll certainly try to make my portraits as true to life[1] as possible. But I'm not entirely[2] sure of succeeding. One drawing works[3], and the next no longer bears[4] any resemblance[5]. And I'm a little off[6] on his height[7], too. In this one the little prince is too tall. And here he's too short. And I'm uncertain about the color of his suit.

So I grope[8] in one direction[9] and another, as best I can. In the end, I'm sure to get certain more important details all wrong. But here you'll have to forgive[10] me. My friend never explained anything. Perhaps he thought I was like himself. But I, unfortunately, cannot see a sheep through the sides of a crate. I may be a little like the grown-ups. I must have grown old.

---

1. **true to life** 逼真的
2. **entirely** [ɪn`taɪrli] (adv.) 完全地；徹底地
3. **work** [wɜːrk] (v.) 起作用
4. **bear** [ber] (v.) 擁有
5. **resemblance** [rɪ`zembləns] (n.) 相似
6. **off** [ɑːf] (a.) 偏離的
7. **height** [haɪt] (n.) 身高
8. **grope** [group] (v.) 摸索
9. **direction** [də`rekʃən] (n.) 方向
10. **forgive** [fər`gɪv] (v.) 原諒；寬恕

The Little Prince on Asteroid B-612

14

5

Every day I'd learn something about the little prince's planet, about his departure[1], about his journey[2]. It would come quite gradually[3], in the course of[4] his remarks[5]. This was how I learned, on the third day, about the drama[6] of the baobabs[7].

This time, too, I had the sheep to thank, for suddenly the little prince asked me a question, as if overcome[8] by a grave[9] doubt.

"Isn't it true that sheep eat bushes[10]?"

"Yes, that's right."

"Ah! I'm glad."

I didn't understand why it was so important that sheep should eat bushes.

But the little prince added:

"And therefore[11] they eat baobabs, too?"

---

1. **departure** [dɪ`pɑ:rtʃər] (n.) 離開；出發
2. **journey** [`dʒɜ:rni] (n.) 旅行
3. **gradually** [`grædʒuəli] (adv.) 逐步地；漸漸地
4. **in the course of** 在……期間
5. **remark** [rɪ`mɑ:rk] (n.) 言詞；談論
6. **drama** [`drɑ:mə] (n.) (一齣)劇；戲劇
7. **baobab** (n.) 猢猻麵包樹

I pointed out[12] to the little prince that baobabs are not bushes but trees as tall as churches, and that even if he took a whole herd[13] of elephants back to his planet, that herd couldn't finish off[14] a single baobab.

The idea of the herd of elephants made the little prince laugh.

"We'd have to pile[15] them on top of one another."

---

8. **overcome** [ˌouvər`kʌm] (v.) 使無法行動或思考 (overcome-overcame-overcome)
9. **grave** [greɪv] (a.) 重大的；認真的
10. **bush** [buʃ] (n.) 灌木
11. **therefore** [`ðerfɔ:r] (adv.) 因此；所以
12. **point out** 指出
13. **herd** [hɜ:rd] (n.) 牧群
14. **finish off** 吃完
15. **pile** [paɪl] (v.) 堆疊；堆積

15

But he observed[1] perceptively[2]:

"Before they grow big, baobabs start out by being little."

"True enough! But why do you want your sheep to eat little baobabs?"

He answered, "Oh, come on! You know!" as if we were talking about something quite obvious[3].

And I was forced to[4] make a great mental[5] effort to understand this problem all by myself.

And, in fact, on the little prince's planet there were — as on all planets — good plants and bad plants. The good plants come from good seeds[6], and the bad plants from bad seeds. But the seeds are invisible[7].

---

1. **observe** [əb`zɜ:rv] (v.) 觀察；注意
2. **perceptively** [pər`septɪvli] (adv.) 敏銳地
3. **obvious** [`ɑ:bviəs] (a.) 明顯的
4. **be forced to** 被迫去
5. **mental** [`mentl] (a.) 精神的；心理的（反義：physical 物質的）
6. **seed** [si:d] (n.) 種子
7. **invisible** [ɪn`vɪzɪbəl] (a.) 看不見的
8. **secrecy** [`si:krəsi] (n.) 秘密；秘密狀態
9. **stretch** [stretʃ] (v.) 伸直；伸出
10. **sprout** [spraut] (v.) 萌芽；生長

They sleep in the secrecy[8] of the ground until one of them decides to wake up. Then it stretches[9] and begins to sprout[10], quite timidly[11] at first, a charming, harmless[12] little twig[13] reaching toward the sun.

If it's a radish[14] seed, or a rosebush seed, you can let it sprout all it likes. But if it's the seed of a bad plant, you must pull the plant up[15] right away, as soon as you can recognize[16] it.

As it happens[17], there were terrible seeds on the little prince's planet . . . baobab seeds. The planet's soil[18] was infested with[19] them. Now if you attend[20] to a baobab too late, you can never get rid of[21] it again.

It overgrows[22] the whole planet.

11. **timidly** [ˋtɪmɪdli] (adv.) 膽小地；羞怯地
12. **harmless** [ˋhɑ:rmləs] (a.) 無害的
13. **twig** [twɪg] (n.) 嫩枝；細枝
14. **radish** [ˋrædɪʃ] (n.) 櫻桃蘿蔔
15. **pull up** 拔；向上拉
16. **recognize** [ˋrekəgnaɪz] (v.) 認出
17. **as it happens** 碰巧
18. **soil** [sɔɪl] (n.) 泥土
19. **be infested with** 被……寄生
20. **attend (to)** 關心；照料
21. **get rid of** 擺脫
22. **overgrow** [ˋoʊvərˏgroʊ] (v.) 生長過快

16 Its roots pierce[1] right through. And if the planet is too small, and if there are too many baobabs, they make it burst into pieces[2].

---

1. **pierce** [pɪrs] (v.) 刺穿
2. **burst into pieces** 爆裂成碎片
3. **discipline** [`dɪsəplɪn] (n.) 紀律；訓練
4. **tend** [tend] (v.) 照料
5. **tell . . . apart** 分辨
6. **resemble** [rɪ`zembəl] (v.) 相似；類似
7. **tedious** [`ti:diəs] (a.) 使人厭煩的；冗長乏味的
8. **advise** [əd`vaɪz] (v.) 勸告；忠告

"It's a question of discipline[3]," the little prince told me later on. "When you've finished washing and dressing each morning, you must tend[4] your planet. You must be sure you pull up the baobabs regularly, as soon as you can tell them apart[5] from the rosebushes, which they closely resemble[6] when they're very young. It's very tedious[7] work, but very easy."

And one day he advised[8] me to do my best to make a beautiful drawing, for the edification[9] of the children where I live.

"If they travel someday," he told me, "it could be useful to them. Sometimes there's no harm in postponing[10] your work until later. But with baobabs, it's always a catastrophe[11]. I knew one planet that was inhabited[12] by a lazy man.

He had neglected[13] three bushes . . ."

---

9. **edification** [ˏedɪfəˋkeɪʃən]
   (n.) 教導
10. **postpone** [poustˋpoun]
   (v.) 使延期
   (= put off, delay)
11. **catastrophe** [kəˋtæstrəfi]
   (n.) 大災；大禍
12. **inhabit** [ɪnˋhæbɪt]
   (v.) 居住於
13. **neglect** [nɪˋglekt]
   (v.) 忽略；忽視

17

So, following the little prince's instructions[1], I have drawn that planet. I don't much like assuming[2] the tone[3] of a moralist[4]. But the danger of baobabs is so little recognized, and the risks run by anyone who might get lost on an asteroid are so considerable[5], that for once I am making an exception[6] to my habitual[7] reserve[8].

I say, "Children, watch out for baobabs!"

It's to warn my friends of a danger[9] of which they, like myself, have long been unaware that I worked so hard on this drawing. The lesson I'm teaching is worth the trouble[10].

You may be asking, "Why are there no other drawings in this book as big as the drawing of the baobabs?" There's a simple answer: I tried but I couldn't manage it. When I drew the baobabs, I was inspired[11] by a sense of urgency[12].

---

1. **instructions** [ɪn`strʌkʃənz] (n.) 指示
2. **assume** [ə`su:m] (v.) 假裝
3. **tone** [toʊn] (n.) 音調；音色
4. **moralist** [`mɔ:rəlɪst] (n.) 道德家；倫理學者
5. **considerable** [kən`sɪdərəbəl] (a.) 相當大的；相當多的
6. **exception** [ɪk`sepʃən] (n.) 例外
7. **habitual** [hə`bɪtʃuəl] (a.) 習慣的；習以為常的
8. **reserve** [rɪ`zɜ:rv] (n.) 含蓄；冷淡
9. **warn A of B** 告誡 A 關於 B
10. **worth the trouble** 值得去做的
11. **inspired** [ɪn`spaɪrd] (a.) 有靈感的
12. **urgency** [`ɜ:rdʒənsi] (n.) 緊急；迫切

The Baobabs

6

Oh Little Prince! Gradually, this was how I came to understand your sad little life. For a long time your only entertainment[1] was the pleasure[2] of sunsets[3]. I learned this new detail on the morning of the fourth day, when you told me:

"I really like sunsets. Let's go look at one now . . ."

"But we have to wait . . ."

"What for?"

"For the sun to set[4]."

At first you seemed quite surprised, and then you laughed at yourself. And you said to me, "I think I'm still at home!"

Indeed. When it's noon in the United States, the sun, as everyone knows, is setting over France. If you could fly to France in one minute, you could watch the sunset. Unfortunately France is much too far. But on your tiny[5] planet, all you had to do was move your chair a few feet. And you would watch the twilight[6] whenever you wanted to . . . .

"One day I saw the sun set forty-four times!" And a little later you added, "You know, when you're feeling very sad, sunsets are wonderful . . ."

"On the day of the forty-four times, were you feeling very sad?"

But the little prince didn't answer.

---

1. **entertainment** [ˏentər`teɪnmənt] (n.) 消遣；娛樂
2. **pleasure** [`pleʒər] (n.) 愉快
3. **sunset** [`sʌnset] (n.) 日落
4. **set** [set] (v.) 下沉 (set-set-set)
5. **tiny** [`taɪni] (a.) 極小的
6. **twilight** [`twaɪlaɪt] (n.) 黄昏

19

7

On the fifth day, thanks again to[1] the sheep, another secret of the little prince's life was revealed[2] to me. Abruptly[3], with no preamble[4], he asked me, as if it were the fruit[5] of a problem long pondered[6] in silence:

"If a sheep eats bushes, does it eat flowers, too?"

"A sheep eats whatever it finds."

"Even flowers that have thorns?"

"Yes. Even flowers that have thorns."

"Then what good are thorns[7]?"

I didn't know. At that moment I was very busy trying to unscrew[8] a bolt that was jammed[9] in my engine. I was quite worried, for my plane crash was beginning to seem extremely serious, and the lack of drinking water made me fear the worst.

---

1. **thanks to** 幸虧；由於
2. **reveal** [rɪ`vi:l] (v.) 顯露出；展現
3. **abruptly** [ə`brʌptli] (adv.) 突然地；意外地
4. **preamble** [`priæmbəl] (n.) 序文；前言
5. **fruit** [fru:t] (n.) 結果
6. **ponder** [`pɑ:ndər] (v.) 沉思；仔細考慮
7. **thorn** [θɔ:rn] (n.) 刺；棘
8. **unscrew** [ʌn`skru:] (v.) 旋出
9. **jam** [dʒæm] (v.) 塞進；擠進
10. **let go of** 放開；釋放

"What good are thorns?"

The little prince never let go of[10] a question once he had asked it. I was annoyed by my jammed bolt, and I answered without thinking.

"Thorns are no good for anything — they're just the flowers' way of being mean[11]!"

"Oh!" But after a silence, he lashed out[12] at me, with a sort of bitterness[13].

"I don't believe you! Flowers are weak. They're naive[14]. They reassure[15] themselves whatever way they can. They believe their thorns make them frightening[16]. . ."

---

11. **mean** [mi:n] (a.)
心地不好的；鄙陋的
12. **lash out** 猛擊
13. **bitterness** [`bɪtərnəs]
(n.) 痛苦；悲痛
14. **naive** [naɪ`i:v] (a.)
天真的；幼稚的
15. **reassure** [ˏri:ə`ʃʊr] (v.)
使放心；向……再保證
16. **frightening** [`fraɪtnɪŋ]
(a.) 使恐懼的；嚇人的

20

I made no answer. At that moment I was thinking, "If this bolt stays jammed, I'll knock it off[1] with the hammer." Again the little prince disturbed[2] my reflections[3].

"Then you think flowers . . ."

"No, not at all. I don't think anything! I just said whatever came into my head. I'm busy here with something serious!"

He stared at me, astounded.

"Something serious!"

1. **knock off** 打掉
2. **disturb** [dɪ`stɜ:rb] (v.) 妨礙；打擾
3. **reflection** [rɪ`flekʃən] (n.) 思考；沉思
4. **grease** [gri:s] (n.) 潤滑脂；油脂
5. **bend over** 折彎過去
6. **regard as** 把⋯⋯視為

He saw me holding my hammer, my fingers black with grease[4], bending over[5] an object he regarded as[6] very ugly.

"You talk like the grown-ups!"

That made me a little ashamed[7].

But he added, mercilessly[8]:

"You confuse everything . . . You've got it all mixed up[9]!" He was really very annoyed. He tossed[10] his golden curls in the wind. "I know a planet inhabited by a red-faced gentleman. He's never smelled a flower. He's never looked at a star. He's never loved anyone. He's never done anything except add up[11] numbers. And all day long he says over and over, just like you, 'I'm a serious man! I'm a serious man!' And that puffs him up[12] with pride. But he's not a man at all — he's a mushroom[13]!"

---

7. **ashamed** [əˋʃeɪmd]
   (a.) 羞愧的
8. **mercilessly** [ˋmɜ:rsɪləsli]
   (adv.) 無情地；殘忍地
9. **mix up** 混雜；使混亂
10. **toss** [tɑ:s] (v.) 拋；投
11. **add up** 把……加起來
12. **puff up**
   使驕傲自大；吹捧
13. **mushroom** [ˋmʌʃrʊm]
   (n.) 蘑菇

21

"He's a what?"

"A mushroom!" The little prince was now quite pale[1] with rage[2]. "For millions of years flowers have been producing thorns. For millions of years sheep have been eating them all the same[3]. And it's not serious, trying to understand why flowers go to such trouble[4] to produce thorns that are good for nothing?

It's not important, the war between the sheep and the flowers? It's no more serious and more important than the numbers that fat red gentleman is adding up?

1. **pale** [peɪl] (a.) 蒼白的
2. **rage** [reɪdʒ] (n.) 狂怒；盛怒
3. **all the same** 還是；依然
4. **go to trouble + to** 拼命；費力（做事）
5. **suppose** [sə`poʊz] (v.) 假設
6. **happen to** 碰巧；偶然
7. **unique** [juː`niːk] (a.) 獨一無二的；獨特的
8. **wipe out** 消滅；徹底摧毀
9. **bite** [baɪt] (n.) 咬
10. **go out** 熄滅

Suppose[5] I happen to[6] know a unique[7] flower, one that exists nowhere in the world except on my planet, one that a little sheep can wipe out[8] in a single bite[9] one morning, just like that, without even realizing what he's doing — that isn't important?"

His face turned red now, and he went on. "If someone loves a flower of which just one example exists among all the millions and millions of stars, that's enough to make him happy when he looks at the stars. He tells himself, 'My flower's up there somewhere . . .' But if the sheep eats the flower, then for him it's as if, suddenly, all the stars went out[10]. And that isn't important?"

22

He couldn't say another word. All of a sudden he burst out sobbing[1]. Night had fallen. I dropped my tools. What did I care about my hammer, about my bolt, about thirst and death? There was, on one star, on one planet, on mine, the Earth, a little prince to be consoled[2]! I took him in my arms. I rocked[3] him. I told him, "The flower you love is not in danger . . . I'll draw you a muzzle[4] for your sheep . . . I'll draw you a fence[5] for your flower . . . I . . ."

I didn't know what to say. How clumsy[6] I felt! I didn't know how to reach him, where to find him . . . . It's so mysterious, the land of tears.

1. **sob** [sɑ:b] (v.)
   嗚咽；啜泣
2. **console** [kən`soul] (v.) 安慰
3. **rock** [rɑ:k] (v.)
   搖動；使搖晃
4. **muzzle** [`mʌzəl] (n.)
   (動物的)口套
5. **fence** [fens] (n.)
   柵欄；籬笆
6. **clumsy** [`klʌmzi] (a.)
   笨拙的；手腳不靈活的
7. **decorated with**
   裝飾著……

8

I soon learned to know that flower better. On the little prince's planet, there had always been very simple flowers, decorated with[7] a single row[8] of petals[9] so that they took up[10] no room at all and got in no one's way. They would appear one morning in the grass, and would fade[11] by nightfall[12].

But this one had grown from a seed brought from who knows where, and the little prince had kept a close watch over a sprout that was not like any of the others. It might have been a new kind of baobab. But the sprout[13] soon stopped growing and began to show signs of blossoming[14].

8. **row** [roʊ] (n.) (一) 列；排
9. **petal** [ˋpetl] (n.) 花瓣
10. **take up** 佔用
11. **fade** [feɪd] (v.) 枯萎；凋謝 (= wither)
12. **nightfall** [ˋnaɪtfɑ:l] (n.) 黃昏；傍晚
13. **sprout** [spraʊt] (n.) 新芽；嫩枝
14. **blossom** [ˋblɑ:səm] (v.) 開花；生長茂盛

23

The little prince, who had watched the development of an enormous[1] bud[2], realized that some sort of miraculous[3] apparition[4] would emerge[5] from it, but the flower continued her beauty preparations in the shelter[6] of her green chamber[7], selecting her colors with the greatest care and dressing quite deliberately[8], adjusting[9] her petals one by one.

She had no desire to emerge all rumpled[10], like the poppies[11]. She wished to appear only in the full radiance[12] of her beauty. Oh yes, she was quite vain[13]! And her mysterious adornment[14] had lasted days and days. And then one morning, precisely[15] at sunrise, she showed herself.

---

1. **enormous** [ɪˋnɔːrməs] (a.) 巨大的；龐大的
2. **bud** [bʌd] (n.) 芽；葉芽
3. **miraculous** [mɪˋrækjʊləs] (a.) 神奇的；超自然的
4. **apparition** [ˏæpəˋrɪʃən] (n.) 特異景象；幽靈
5. **emerge** [ɪˋmɜːrdʒ] (v.) 浮現；出現
6. **shelter** [ˋʃeltər] (n.) 遮蓋物；躲避物
7. **chamber** [ˋtʃeɪmbər] (n.) 室；房間
8. **deliberately** [dɪˋlɪbərətli] (adv.) 慎重地；謹慎地
9. **adjust** [əˋdʒʌst] (v.) 調節；改變
10. **rumpled** [ˋrʌmpəld] (a.) 弄皺的；凌亂的
11. **poppy** [ˋpɑːpi] (n.) 罌粟
12. **radiance** [ˋreɪdiəns] (n.) 光輝
13. **vain** [veɪn] (a.) 愛虛榮的；自負的
14. **adornment** [əˋdɔːrnmənt] (n.) 裝飾品
15. **precisely** [prɪˋsaɪsli] (adv.) 精準地；準確地

And after having labored[16] so painstakingly[17], she yawned[18] and said, "Ah! I'm hardly awake . . . Forgive me . . . I'm still all untidy . . ."

But the little prince couldn't contain[19] his admiration.

"How lovely you are!"

"Aren't I?" the flower answered sweetly. "And I was born the same time as the sun . . ."

The little prince realized that she wasn't any too modest[20], but she was so dazzling[21]!

"I believe it is breakfast time," she had soon added. "Would you be so kind as to tend to me?"

And the little prince, utterly[22] abashed[23], having gone to look for a watering can, served the flower.

---

16. **labor** [ˋleɪbər] (v.) 勞動；艱苦地幹活
17. **painstakingly** [ˋpeɪnzˏteɪkɪŋli] (adv.) 刻苦地；煞費苦心地
18. **yawn** [jɑːn] (v.) 打呵欠
19. **contain** [kənˋteɪn] (v.) 控制（情緒）
20. **modest** [ˋmɑːdɪst] (a.) 端莊的；審慎的
21. **dazzling** [ˋdæzəlɪŋ] (a.) 燦爛的；耀眼的
22. **utterly** [ˋʌtərli] (adv.) 完全地；徹底地
23. **abashed** [əˋbæʃt] (a.) 窘的；尷尬的

She had soon begun tormenting[1] him with her rather touchy[2] vanity[3]. One day, for instance, alluding[4] to her four thorns, she remarked to the little prince, "I'm ready for tigers, with all their claws[5]!"

"There are no tigers on my planet," the little prince had objected[6], "and besides, tigers don't eat weeds[7]."

"I am not a weed," the flower sweetly replied.

"Forgive me . . ."

---

1. **torment** [ˋtɔ:rment] (v.) 使痛苦；折磨
2. **touchy** [ˋtʌtʃi] (a.) 易怒的；棘手的
3. **vanity** [ˋvænəti] (n.) 自負；虛榮（心）
4. **allude** [əˋlu:d] (v.) 暗示；間接提到
5. **claw** [klɑ:] (n.) 爪子
6. **object** [əbˋdʒekt] (v.) 反對
7. **weed** [wi:d] (n.) 雜草
8. **draft** [dræft] (n.) 冷空氣
9. **screen** [skri:n] (n.) 屏；幕
10. **horror** [ˋhɔ:rər] (n.) 恐懼
11. **observe** [əbˋzɜ:rv] (v.) 注意；觀察

"I am not at all afraid of tigers, but I have a horror of drafts[8]. You wouldn't happen to have a screen[9]?"

"A horror[10] of drafts. . . that's not a good sign, for a plant," the little prince had observed[11]. "How complicated[12] this flower is . . ."

"After dark you will put me under glass. How cold it is where you live — quite uncomfortable. Where I come from—" But she suddenly broke off[13]. She had come here as a seed. She couldn't have known anything of other worlds.

Humiliated[14] at having let herself be caught on the verge of[15] so naive a lie, she coughed[16] two or three times in order to put the little prince in the wrong[17]. "That screen?"

---

12. **complicated**
[ˋkɑ:mplɪkeɪtɪd]
(a.) 難懂的；複雜的
13. **break off** 突然停止；中斷
14. **humiliate** [hju:ˋmɪlieɪt]
(v.) 使蒙羞；丟臉
15. **on the verge of**
接近於；瀕於
16. **cough** [kɑ:f] (v.) 咳嗽
17. **put A in the wrong**
讓 A 承受錯誤；
讓 A 感受責備

25

"I was going to look for one, but you were speaking to me!"

Then she made herself cough again, in order to inflict[1] a twinge[2] of remorse[3] on him all the same.

So the little prince, despite all the goodwill[4] of his love, had soon come to mistrust[5] her. He had taken seriously certain inconsequential[6] remarks and had grown very unhappy.

1. **inflict** [ɪn`flɪkt] (v.) 給予；使遭受
2. **twinge** [twɪndʒ] (n.) 內疚；難過
3. **remorse** [rɪ`mɔ:rs] (n.) 自責；痛悔
4. **goodwill** [`gʊd`wɪl] (n.) 好意；善意
5. **mistrust** [mɪs`trʌst] (v.) 不信任；懷疑

"I shouldn't have listened to her," he confided[7] to me one day. "You must never listen to flowers. You must look at them and smell them. Mine perfumed[8] my planet, but I didn't know how to enjoy that. The business about the tiger claws, instead of annoying me, ought to have moved me . . ."

And he confided further[9], "In those days, I didn't understand anything. I should have judged[10] her according to her actions, not her words. She perfumed my planet and lit up my life. I should never have run away! I ought to have realized the tenderness underlying[11] her silly pretensions[12].
Flowers are so contradictory[13]! But I was too young to know how to love her."

---

6. **inconsequential** [ɪnˏkɑ:nsɪˋkwenʃəl] (a.) 不合理的
7. **confide** [kənˋfaɪd] (v.) 透露
8. **perfume** [pɜ:rˋfju:m] (v.) 使充滿香氣
9. **further** [ˋfɜ:rðər] (adv.) 進一步地
10. **judge** [dʒʌdʒ] (v.) 評斷
11. **underlie** [ˏʌndərˋlaɪ] (v.) 隱藏在……之下
12. **pretension** [prɪˋtenʃən] (n.) 藉口；托詞
13. **contradictory** [ˏkɑ:ntrəˋdɪktəri] (a.) 矛盾的

9

26

In order to make his escape[1], I believe he took advantage of[2] a migration[3] of wild birds. On the morning of his departure[4], he put his planet in order[5]. He carefully raked out[6] his active volcanoes[7]. The little prince possessed two active volcanoes, which were very convenient[8] for warming his breakfast.

He also possessed[9] one extinct volcano[10]. But, as he said, "You never know!"

So he raked out the extinct volcano, too. If they are properly[11] raked out, volcanoes burn gently and regularly, without eruptions[12]. Volcanic eruptions are like fires in a chimney[13].

---

1. **make one's escape** 使某人逃離
2. **take advantage of** 利用；佔便宜
3. **migration** [maɪˋgreɪʃən] (n.) 遷徙
4. **departure** [dɪˋpɑːrtʃər] (n.) 離開；出發
5. **put in order** 使有秩序；使有條理
6. **rake out** 搜出
7. **active volcano** 活火山
8. **convenient** [kənˋviːniənt] (a.) 方便的
9. **possess** [pəˋzes] (v.) 擁有；持有
10. **extinct volcano** 死火山
11. **properly** [ˋprɑːpərli] (adv.) 恰當地；正確地

Of course, on our Earth we are much too small to rake out our volcanoes. That is why they cause us so much trouble.

The little prince also uprooted[14], a little sadly, the last baobab shoots[15]. He believed he would never be coming back. But all these familiar[16] tasks[17] seemed very sweet to him on this last morning. And when he watered the flower one last time, and put her under glass, he felt like crying[18].

"Good-bye," he said to the flower.

But she did not answer him.

"Good-bye," he repeated.

The flower coughed. But not because she had a cold.

---

12. **eruption** [ɪ`rʌpʃən] (n.) (火山)爆發；(熔岩的)噴出
13. **chimney** [`tʃɪmni] (n.) 煙囪
14. **uproot** [ʌp`ru:t] (v.) 連根拔除
15. **shoot** [ʃu:t] (n.) 嫩芽
16. **familiar** [fə`mɪliər] (a.) 熟悉的；常見的
17. **task** [tæsk] (n.) 工作；任務
18. **feel like + V-ing** 想要去做……

27

"I've been silly," she told him at last. "I ask your forgiveness. Try to be happy."

He was surprised that there were no reproaches[1]. He stood there, quite bewildered[2], holding the glass bell in midair[3]. He failed to understand this calm sweetness.

"Of course I love you," the flower told him. "It was my fault you never knew. It doesn't matter. But you were just as silly as I was. Try to be happy . . . Put that glass thing down. I don't want it anymore."

---

1. **reproach** [rɪˋproutʃ] (v.) 責備；斥責
2. **bewildered** [bɪˋwɪldərd] (a.) 困惑的
3. **midair** [mɪdˋer] (n.) 半空中
4. **do good** 對……有好處
5. **put up with** 忍受；容忍
6. **caterpillar** [ˋkætər͵pɪlər] (n.) 毛毛蟲
7. **get to know** 去認識

"But the wind . . ."

"My cold isn't that bad . . . The night air will do me good[4]. I'm a flower."

"But the animals . . ."

"I need to put up with[5] two or three caterpillars[6] if I want to get to know[7] the butterflies. Apparently[8] they're very beautiful. Otherwise[9] who will visit me? You'll be far away. As for the big animals, I'm not afraid of them. I have my own claws." And she naively showed her four thorns.

Then she added, "Don't hang around[10] like this; it's irritating[11]. You made up your mind[12] to leave. Now go."

For she didn't want him to see her crying. She was such a proud flower . . . .

---

8. **apparently** [ə`pærəntli]
   (adv.) 顯然地
9. **otherwise** [`ʌðərwaɪz]
   (adv.) 否則；不然
10. **hang around** 徘徊
11. **irritating** [`ɪrɪteɪtɪŋ]
    (a.) 使人惱怒的
12. **make up one's mind**
    下定決心 (= decide)

He carefully raked out his active volcanoes.

28

10

He happened to be in the vicinity[1] of Asteroids 325, 326, 327, 328, 329, and 330. So he began by visiting them, to keep himself busy and to learn something.

The first one was inhabited by a king. Wearing purple and ermine[2], he was sitting on a simple yet majestic[3] throne[4].

"Ah! Here's a subject[5]!" the king exclaimed when he caught sight of[6] the little prince.

And the little prince wondered, "How can he know who I am if he's never seen me before?" He didn't realize that for kings, the world is extremely[7] simplified[8]: All men are subjects.

1. **vicinity** [və`sɪnəti] (n.) 附近地區；近鄰
2. **ermine** [`ɜ:rmɪn] (n.) 貂皮
3. **majestic** [mə`dʒestɪk] (a.) 威嚴的；崇高的
4. **throne** [θroʊn] (n.) 寶座；御座
5. **subject** [`sʌbdʒɪkt] (n.) 國民；臣民
6. **catch sight of** 看到
7. **extremely** [ɪk`stri:mli] (adv.) 非常地；極端地
8. **simplify** [`sɪmpləfaɪ] (v.) 簡化

"Approach[1] the throne so I can get a better look at you," said the king, very proud of being a king for someone at last.

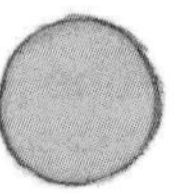

The little prince looked around for a place to sit down, but the planet was covered by the magnificent ermine cloak[2]. So he remained[3] standing, and since he was tired, he yawned.

"It is a violation[4] of etiquette to yawn in a king's presence," the monarch[5] told him. "I forbid[6] you to do so."

"I can't help it[7]," answered the little prince, quite embarrassed. "I've made a long journey, and I haven't had any sleep . . ."

"Then I command[8] you to yawn," said the king. "I haven't seen anyone yawn for years. For me, yawns are a curiosity[9]. Come on, yawn again! It is an order."

"That intimidates[10] me . . . I can't do it now," said the little prince, blushing[12] deeply.

---

1. **approach** [ə`proutʃ] (v.) 靠近；接近
2. **cloak** [klouk] (n.) 斗篷；披風
3. **remain** [rɪ`meɪn] (v.) 保持；仍是
4. **violation** [ˏvaɪə`leɪʃən] (n.) 違反的行為舉止
5. **monarch** [`mɑ:nərk] (n.) 君主
6. **forbid** [fər`bɪd] (v.) 禁止；不許
7. **cannot help it** 不得不
8. **command** [kə`mænd] (v.) 命令
9. **curiosity** [ˏkjʊri`ɑ:səti] (n.) 罕見事物
10. **intimidate** [ɪn`tɪmədeɪt] (v.) 威嚇；脅迫
11. **blush** [blʌʃ] (v.) 臉紅

30

"Well, well!" the king replied. "Then I . . . I command you to yawn sometimes and sometimes to . . ."

He was sputtering[1] a little, and seemed annoyed[2], for the king insisted[3] that his authority[4] be universally[5] respected. He would tolerate[6] no disobedience[7], being an absolute[8] monarch. But since he was a kindly man, all his commands were reasonable[9].

"If I were to command," he would often say, "if I were to command a general to turn into[10] a seagull[11], and if the general did not obey, that would not be the general's fault. It would be mine."

"May I sit down?" the little prince timidly inquired[12].

1. **sputter** [ˋspʌtər] (v.) 結結巴巴地說
2. **annoyed** [əˋnɔɪd] (a.) 惱怒的；氣惱的
3. **insist** [ɪnˋsɪst] (v.) 堅持；堅決認為
4. **authority** [əˋqɔ:rəti] (n.) 權力；威信
5. **universally** [ˏju:nɪˋvɜ:rsəli] (adv.) 普遍地；一般地
6. **tolerate** [ˋtɑ:ləreɪt] (v.) 容忍；寬恕
7. **disobedience** [ˏdɪsəˋbi:diəns] (n.) 不服從；違抗

"I command you to sit down," the king replied, majestically gathering up[13] a fold[14] of his ermine robe.

But the little prince was wondering. The planet was tiny. Over what could the king really reign[15]? "Sire[16] . . . ," he ventured[17], "excuse me for asking . . ."

"I command you to ask," the king hastened[18] to say.

"Sire . . . over what do you reign?"

"Over everything," the king answered, with great simplicity.

"Over everything?"

With a discreet[19] gesture the king pointed to his planet, to the other planets, and to the stars.

"Over all that?" asked the little prince.

---

8. **absolute** [ˋæbsəlu:t] (a.) 純粹的；完全的
9. **reasonable** [ˋri:zənəbəl] (a.) 通情達理的
10. **turn into** 使變成
11. **seagull** [ˋsi:ˋgʌl] (n.) 海鷗 (= sea gull)
12. **inquire** [ɪnˋkwaɪr] (v.) 詢問
13. **gather up** 聚集
14. **fold** [fould] (n.) 摺疊
15. **reign** [reɪn] (v.) 統治；支配
16. **Sire** [saɪr] (n.) 陛下
17. **venture** [ˋventʃər] (v.) 大膽行事；冒險
18. **hasten** [ˋheɪsən] (v.) 趕緊
19. **discreet** [dɪˋskri:t] (a.) 謹慎的；考慮周全的

31

"Over all that . . . ," the king answered.

For not only was he an absolute monarch, but a universal monarch as well.

"And do the stars obey you?"

"Of course," the king replied. "They obey immediately. I tolerate no insubordination[1]."

Such power amazed the little prince. If he had wielded[2] it himself, he could have watched not forty-four but seventy-two, or even a hundred, even two hundred sunsets on the same day without ever having to move his chair! And since he was feeling rather sad on account of remembering his own little planet, which he had forsaken[3], he ventured to ask a favor[4] of the king:

"I'd like to see a sunset . . . Do me a favor, your majesty . . . Command the sun to set . . ."

1. **insubordination** [ˋɪnsəˏbɔ:rdɪˋneɪʃən] (n.) 不順從
2. **wield** [wi:ld] (v.) 行使（權力）
3. **forsake** [fərˋseɪk] (v.) 拋棄；遺棄 (forsake-forsook-forsaken)
4. **favor** [ˋfeɪvər] (n.) 支持；贊同

"If I commanded a general to fly from one flower to the next like a butterfly, or to write a tragedy[5], or to turn into a seagull, and if the general[6] did not carry out[7] my command, which of us would be in the wrong, the general or me?"

"You would be," said the little prince, quite firmly[8].

"Exactly. One must command from each what each can perform," the king went on. "Authority is based first of all upon[9] reason. If you command your subjects to jump in the ocean, there will be a revolution[10]. I am entitled[11] to command obedience[12] because my orders are reasonable."

"Then my sunset?" insisted the little prince, who never let go of a question once he had asked it.

---

5. **tragedy** [ˋtrædʒədi] (n.) 悲劇
6. **general** [ˋdʒenərəl] (n.) 將軍
7. **carry out** 完成；實行
8. **firmly** [ˋfɜ:rmli] (adv.) 堅決地；堅定地
9. **be based upon(on)** 建立在……之上
10. **revolution** [ˏrevəˋlu:ʃən] (n.) 革命
11. **be entitled to** 被授予權力去……
12. **obedience** [əˋbi:diəns] (n.) 服從

32

"You shall have your sunset. I shall command it. But I shall wait, according to[1] my science of government, until conditions[2] are favorable[3]."

"And when will that be?" inquired the little prince.

"Well, well!" replied the king, first consulting[4] a large calendar. "Well, well! That will be around . . . around . . . that will be tonight around seven-forty! And you'll see how well I am obeyed."

The little prince yawned. He was regretting[5] his lost sunset. And besides[6], he was already growing a little bored. "I have nothing further to do here," he told the king. "I'm going to be on my way!"

"Do not leave!" answered the king, who was so proud of having a subject. "Do not leave; I shall make you my minister[7]!"

---

1. **according to** 根據；按照
2. **condition** [kən`dɪʃən] (n.) 情況；狀態
3. **favorable** [`feɪvərəbəl] (a.) 適合的
4. **consult** [kən`sʌlt] (v.) 查閱
5. **regret** [rɪ`gret] (v.) 感到遺憾
6. **besides** [bɪ`saɪdz] (adv.) 此外；而且
7. **minister** [`mɪnɪstər] (n.) 部長；大臣
8. **the Minister of Justice** 司法部部長
9. **judge** [dʒʌdʒ] (v.) 審判；判決

"A minister of what?"

"Of . . . of justice[8].

"But there's no one here to judge[9]!"

"You never know," the king told him. "I have not yet explored[10] the whole of my realm[11]. I am very old, I have no room[12] for a carriage[13], and it wearies[14] me to walk."

"Oh, but I've already seen for myself," said the little prince, leaning forward[15] to glance[16] one more time at the other side of the planet. "There's no one over there, either . . ."

"Then you shall pass judgment on[17] yourself," the king answered. "That is the hardest thing of all. It is much harder to judge yourself than to judge others. If you succeed in judging yourself, it's because you are truly a wise man."

---

10. **explore** [ɪk`splɔːr] (v.) 探險；探勘
11. **realm** [relm] (n.) 王土；國土
12. **room** [rʊm] (n.) 空間
13. **carriage** [`kærɪdʒ] (n.) 四輪馬車
14. **weary** [`wɪri] (v.) 使疲倦
15. **lean forward** 向前傾靠
16. **glance** [glæns] (v.) 掃視；(略地)看一下
17. **pass judgement on** 審判……

33

"But I can judge myself anywhere," said the little prince. "I don't need to live here."

"Well, well!" the king said. "I have good reason to believe that there is an old rat living somewhere on my planet. I hear him at night. You could judge that old rat. From time to time you will condemn[1] him to death.

That way his life will depend on[2] your justice. But you'll pardon[3] him each time for economy's sake[4]. There's only one rat."

"I don't like condemning anyone to death," the little prince said, "and now I think I'll be on my way."

"No," said the king.

1. **condemn** [kən`dem] (v.) 責難；譴責
2. **depend on** 依賴；信賴
3. **pardon** [`pɑ:rdn] (v.) 饒恕；寬恕
4. **for A's sake** 因為 A 的緣故
5. **aggrieve** [ə`gri:v] (v.) 使悲痛；使受屈
6. **Your Majesty** 陛下
7. **promptly** [`prɑ:mptli] (adv.) 迅速地

The little prince, having completed his preparations, had no desire to aggrieve[5] the old monarch. "If Your Majesty[6] desires to be promptly[7] obeyed, he should give me a reasonable command. He might command me, for instance, to leave before this minute is up. It seems to me that conditions are favorable. . ."

The king having made no answer, the little prince hesitated[8] at first, and then, with a sigh[9], took his leave.

"I make you my ambassador[10]," the king hastily[11] shouted after him. He had a great air of authority.

"Grown-ups are so strange," the little prince said to himself as he went on his way.

8. **hesitate** [`hezəteɪt]
 (v.) 猶豫；躊躇
9. **sigh** [saɪ] (n.) 嘆息
10. **ambassador** [æm`bæsədər]
 (n.) 大使
11. **hastily** [`heɪstəli]
 (adv.) 倉促地；匆忙地

34

11

The second planet was inhabited by a very vain man.

"Ah! A visit from an admirer[1]!" he exclaimed when he caught sight of the little prince, still at some distance[2]. To vain men, other people are admirers.

"Hello," said the little prince. "That's a funny hat you're wearing."

"It's for answering acclamations[3]," the very vain man replied. "Unfortunately, no one ever comes this way."

---

1. **admirer** [əd`maɪrər] (n.) 讚頌者；欽佩者
2. **at some distance** 在一些距離之外
3. **acclamation** [ˏæklə`meɪʃən] (n.) (公開地) 歡呼讚譽
4. **clap one's hands** 鼓掌
5. **direct** [də`rekt] (v.) 命令；指揮
6. **tip** [tɪp] (v.) 脫帽打招呼
7. **modest** [`mɑ:dɪst] (a.) 謙虛的；審慎的
8. **acknowledgment** [ək`nɑ:lɪdʒmənt] (n.) 答謝
9. **entertaining** [ˏentər`teɪnɪŋ] (a.) 使人愉快的；有趣的
10. **tire of** 厭煩
11. **monotony** [mə`nɑ:təni] (n.) 單調；無變化
12. **praise** [preɪz] (n.) 讚揚；稱讚

"Is that so?" said the little prince, who did not understand what the vain man was talking about.

"Clap your hands[4]," directed[5] the man.

The little prince clapped his hands, and the vain man tipped[6] his hat in modest[7] acknowledgment[8].

"This is more entertaining[9] than the visit to the king," the little prince said to himself. And he continued clapping. The very vain man continued tipping his hat in acknowledgment.

After five minutes of this exercise, the little prince tired[10] of the game's monotony[11]. "And what would make the hat fall off?" he asked.

But the vain man did not hear him. Vain men never hear anything but praise[12].

35

"Do you really admire me a great deal[1]?" he asked the little prince.

"What does that mean — *admire*?"

"To *admire* means to acknowledge[2] that I am the handsomest, the best-dressed, the richest, and the most intelligent man on the planet."

"But you're the only man on your planet!"

"Do me this favor[3]. Admire me all the same."

"I admire you," said the little prince, with a little shrug of his shoulders, "but what is there about my admiration that interests you so much?" And the little prince went on his way.

"Grown-ups are certainly very strange," he said to himself as he continued on his journey.

---

1. **a great deal** 大量；非常
2. **acknowledge** [əkˋnɑ:lɪdʒ] (v.) 承認
3. **do A a favor** 幫 A 一個忙
4. **drunkard** [ˋdrʌŋkərd] (n.) 醉漢；酒鬼
5. **brief** [bri:f] (a.) 短暫的
6. **plunge** [plʌndʒ] (v.) 使遭受；使陷入
7. **depression** [dɪˋpreʃən] (n.) 沮喪；意志消沉
8. **sink** [sɪŋk] (v.) 墮落；消沉 (sink-sank-sunk)
9. **gloomy** [ˋglu:mi] (a.) 陰沉的
10. **expression** [ɪkˋspreʃən] (n.) 表情；臉色

12

The next planet was inhabited by a drunkard[4]. This visit was a very brief[5] one, but it plunged[6] the little prince into a deep depression[7].

"What are you doing there?" he asked the drunkard, whom he found sunk[8] in silence before a collection of empty bottles and a collection of full ones.

"Drinking," replied the drunkard, with a gloomy[9] expression[10].

"Why are you drinking?" the little prince asked.

"To forget," replied the drunkard.

"To forget what?" inquired the little prince, who was already feeling sorry for[1] him.

"To forget that I'm ashamed[2]," confessed[3] the drunkard, hanging his head[4].

"What are you ashamed of?" inquired the little prince, who wanted to help.

"Of drinking!" concluded[5] the drunkard, withdrawing into[6] silence for good[7]. And the little prince went on his way, puzzled[8].

"Grown-ups are certainly very, very strange," he said to himself as he continued on his journey.

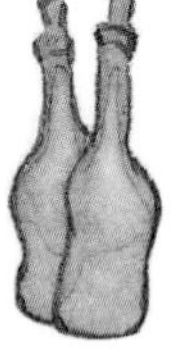

1. **feel sorry for**
   為……感到難過
2. **ashamed** [ə`ʃeɪmd] (a.)
   羞愧的；感到難為情的
3. **confess** [kən`fes]
   (v.) 坦白；承認
4. **hang one's head**
   低垂著頭
5. **conclude** [kən`klu:d]
   (v.) 斷定；推斷

13

The fourth planet belonged to[9] a businessman. This person was so busy that he didn't even raise his head when the little prince arrived.

"Hello," said the little prince. "Your cigarette's gone out."

"Three and two make five. Five and seven, twelve. Twelve and three, fifteen. Hello. Fifteen and seven, twenty-two. Twenty-two and six, twenty-eight. No time to light[10] it again. Twenty-six and five, thirty-one. Whew! That amounts to[11] five-hundred-and-one million, six hundred-twenty-two thousand, seven hundred thirty-one."

"Five-hundred million what?"

---

6. **withdraw** [wɪð`drɑː] (v.) 抽回；收回
   withdraw into 沉默
7. **for good** 永久地
8. **puzzled** [`pʌzəld] (a.) 困惑的
9. **belong to** 屬於……
10. **light** [laɪt] (v.) 點燃 (light-lit-lit)
11. **amount to** 總計為

"Hmm? You're still there? Five-hundred-and-one million . . . I don't remember . . . I have so much work to do! I'm a serious man. I can't be bothered[1] with trifles[2]! Two and five, seven . . ."

"Five-hundred-and-one million what?" repeated the little prince, who had never in his life let go of[3] a question once he had asked it.

The businessman raised his head.

"For the fifty-four years I've inhabited this planet, I've been interrupted[4] only three times. The first time was twenty-two years ago, when I was interrupted by a beetle[5] that had fallen onto my desk from god knows[6] where. It made a terrible noise, and I made four mistakes in my calculations[7]. The second time was eleven years ago, when I was interrupted by a fit[8] of rheumatism[9]. I don't get enough exercise.

I haven't time to take strolls[10]. I'm a serious person. The third time . . . is right now! Where was I? Five hundred-and-one million . . ."

"Million what?"

1. **bother** [ˋbɑ:ðər] (v.) 打擾
2. **trifle** [ˋtraɪfəl] (n.) 瑣事
3. **let go of** 放手；放開
4. **interrupt** [ˏɪntəˋrʌpt] (v.) 打斷
5. **beetle** [ˋbi:tl] (n.) 甲蟲
6. **god knows** 天知道
7. **calculation** [ˏkælkjʊˋleɪʃən] (n.) 計算
8. **fit** [fɪt] (n.) (病的) 發作
9. **rheumatism** [ˋru:mətɪzəm] (n.) 風濕病
10. **take a stroll** 散步；閒逛

38

The businessman realized that he had no hope of being left in peace[1].

"Oh, of those little things you sometimes see in the sky."

"Flies[2]?"

"No, those little shiny[3] things."

"Bees?"

"No, those little golden things that make lazy people daydream[4]. Now, I'm a serious person. I have no time for daydreaming."

"Ah! You mean the stars?"

"Yes, that's it. Stars."

"And what do you do with five-hundred million stars?"

"Five-hundred-and-one million, six-hundred-twenty-two thousand, seven hundred thirty-one. I'm a serious person, and I'm accurate[5]."

“And what do you do with those stars?”

“What do I do with them?”

“Yes.”

“Nothing. I own[6] them.”

“You own the stars?”

“Yes.”

“But I’ve already seen a king who — ”

“Kings don’t own. They ‘reign’ over . . . It’s quite different.”

“And what good does owning the stars do you?”

“It does me the good of being rich.”

“And what good does it do you to be rich?”

“It lets me buy other stars, if somebody discovers them.”

---

1. **in peace** 安心
2. **fly** [flaɪ] (n.) 蒼蠅
3. **shiny** [`ʃaɪni] (a.) 發光的；閃光的
4. **daydream** [`deɪdriːm] (v.) 做白日夢
5. **accurate** [`ækjʊrət] (a.) 精準的；準確的
6. **own** [oʊn] (v.) 擁有

39

The little prince said to himself, "This man argues a little like my drunkard." Nevertheless[1] he asked more questions. "How can someone own the stars?"

"To whom do they belong?" retorted[2] the businessman grumpily[3].

"I don't know. To nobody."

"Then they belong to me, because I thought of it first."

"And that's all it takes?"

"Of course. When you find a diamond that belongs to nobody in particular[4], then it's yours. When you find an island that belongs to nobody in particular, it's yours. When you're the first person to have an idea, you patent[5] it and it's yours. Now I own the stars, since no one before me ever thought of owning them."

1. **nevertheless** [ˌnevərðəˋles] (adv.) 仍然；然而
2. **retort** [rɪˋtɔ:rt] (v.) 反駁
3. **grumpily** [ˋgrʌmpili] (adv.) 暴躁地
4. **in particular** 特別地
5. **patent** [ˋpætnt] (v.) 擁有……的專利

"That's true enough[6]," the little prince said. "And what do you do with them?"

"I manage[7] them. I count them and then count them again," the businessman said. "It's difficult work. But I'm a serious person!"

The little prince was still not satisfied. "If I own a scarf, I can tie[8] it around my neck and take it away[9]. If I own a flower, I can pick[10] it and take it away. But you can't pick the stars!"

"No, but I can put them in the bank."

"What does that mean?"

"That means that I write the number of my stars on a slip[11] of paper. And then I lock that slip of paper in a drawer[12]."

"And that's all?"

"That's enough!"

6. **enough** [ɪˋnʌf] (adv.) 充分地；足夠地
7. **manage** [ˋmænɪdʒ] (v.) 管理
8. **tie** [taɪ] (v.) 繫；紮
9. **take away** 帶走；拿走
10. **pick** [pɪk] (v.) 摘；採
11. **slip** [slɪp] (n.) 紙條；片條
12. **drawer** [ˋdrɑːr] (n.) 抽屜

40

"That's amusing[1]," thought the little prince. "And even poetic[2]. But not very serious." The little prince had very different ideas about serious things from those of the grown-ups.

"I own a flower myself," he continued, "which I water every day. I own three volcanoes, which I rake out every week. I even rake out the extinct one. You never know. So it's of some use[3] to my volcanoes, and it's useful to my flower, that I own them. But you're not useful to the stars."

The businessman opened his mouth but found nothing to say in reply, and the little prince went on his way.

"Grown-ups are certainly quite extraordinary[4]," was all he said to himself as he continued on his journey.

---

1. **amusing** [ə`mju:zɪŋ] (a.) 有趣的；好玩的
2. **poetic** [poʊ`etɪk] (a.) 有詩意的；有想像力的
3. **be of some use** 派上一些用場
4. **extraordinary** [ɪk`strɔ:rdneri] (a.) 奇怪的
5. **street lamp** 街燈
6. **lamplighter** [`læmp͵laɪtər] (n.) 點街燈伕

14

The fifth planet was very strange. It was the smallest of all. There was just enough room for a street lamp[5] and a lamplighter[6]. The little prince couldn't quite understand what use a street lamp and a lamplighter could be up there in the sky, on a planet without any people and not a single house.

However, he said to himself, "It's quite possible that this man is absurd[7], But he's less absurd than the king, the very vain man, the businessman, and the drunkard.

At least his work has some meaning. When he lights his lamp, it's as if he's bringing one more star to life, or one more flower. When he puts out[8] his lamp, that sends the flower or the star to sleep. Which is a fine[9] occupation[10].

And therefore truly useful."

---

7. **absurd** [əb`sɜ:rd] (a.) 不合理的；荒謬的
8. **put out** 熄滅
9. **fine** [faɪn] (a.) 美好的
10. **occupation** [ˏɑ:kjʊ`peɪʃən] (n.) 工作；職業

41

When the little prince reached[1] this planet, he greeted[2] the lamplighter respectfully[3].

"Good morning. Why have you just put out your lamp?"

"Orders[4]," the lamplighter answered. "Good morning."

"What orders are those?"

"To put out my street lamp. Good evening."

And he lit his lamp again.

"But why have you just lit your lamp again?"

"Orders."

"I don't understand," said the little prince.

"There's nothing to understand," said the lamplighter. "Orders are orders. Good morning."

And he put out his lamp. Then he wiped[5] his forehead[6] with a red-checked[7] handkerchief[8].

---

1. **reach** [ri:tʃ] (v.) 抵達；到達
2. **greet** [gri:t] (v.) 問候
3. **respectfully** [rɪ`spektfəli] (adv.) 恭敬地
4. **order** [`ɔ:rdər] (n.) 命令；指示
5. **wipe** [waɪp] (v.) 抹；擦
6. **forehead** [`fɔ:rhed] (n.) 額頭
7. **red-checked** (a.) 紅格子花紋的
8. **handkerchief** [`hæŋkərtʃɪf] (n.) 手帕

"It's a terrible job I have."

"It's a terrible job I have.

It used to[1] be reasonable enough. I put the lamp out mornings and lit it after dark. I had the rest of the day for my own affairs[2], and the rest of the night for sleeping."

"And since then orders have changed?"

"Orders haven't changed," the lamplighter said. "That's just the trouble! Year by year[3] the planet is turning faster and faster, and orders haven't changed!"

"Which means?"

"Which means that now that the planet revolves[4] once a minute, I don't have an instant's[5] rest.

I light my lamp and turn it out once every minute!"

1. **used to** 曾經
2. **affair** [ə`fer] (n.) 事情
3. **year by year** 一年又一年
4. **revolve** [rɪ`vɑ:lv] (v.) 旋轉
5. **instant** [`ɪnstənt] (n.) 一瞬間；頃刻

"That's funny! Your days here are one minute long!"

"It's not funny at all," the lamplighter said. "You and I have already been talking to each other for a month."

"A month?"

"Yes. Thirty minutes. Thirty days! Good evening." And he lit his lamp.

The little prince watched him, growing fonder and fonder of[6] this lamplighter who was so faithful[7] to orders. He remembered certain sunsets that he himself used to follow in other days, merely[8] by shifting[9] his chair. He wanted to help his friend.

---

6. **fond of** 喜歡
7. **faithful** [`feɪθfəl] (a.) 忠實的；忠貞的
8. **merely** [`mɪrli] (adv.) 只是；僅僅
9. **shift** [ʃɪft] (v.) 搬 ；移

"You know . . . I can show you a way to take a rest[1] whenever you want to."

"I always want to rest," the lamplighter said, for it is possible to be faithful and lazy at the same time.

The little prince continued, "Your planet is so small that you can walk around it in three strides[2]. All you have to do is walk more slowly, and you'll always be in the sun. When you want to take a rest just walk . . . and the day will last as long as you want it to."

"What good does that do me?" the lamplighter said, "when the one thing in life I want to do is sleep?"

"Then you're out of luck[3]," said the little prince.

"I am," said the lamplighter. "Good morning." And he put out his lamp.

"Now that man," the little prince said to himself as he continued on his journey, "that man would be despised[4] by all the others, by the king, by the very vain man, by the drunkard, by the businessman. Yet he's the only one who doesn't strike[5] me as ridiculous[6]. Perhaps it's because he's thinking of something beside[7] himself." He heaved a sigh[8] of regret and said to himself, again, "That man is the only one I might have made my friend. But his planet is really too small. There's not room for two . . ."

What the little prince dared[9] not admit[10] was that he most regretted leaving that planet because it was blessed[11] with one thousand, four hundred forty sunsets every twenty-four hours!

---

1. **take a rest** 休息一下
2. **stride** [straɪd] (n.) 闊步；(一)大步
3. **out of luck** 運氣不佳
4. **despise** [dɪ`spaɪz] (v.) 鄙視
5. **strike** [straɪk] (v.) 給……以印象
6. **ridiculous** [rɪ`dɪkjʊləs] (a.) 可笑的；荒謬的
7. **beside** [bɪ`saɪd] (prep.) 除了……以外
8. **have a sigh** 發出嘆息
9. **dare** [der] (v.) 膽敢；竟敢
10. **admit** [ad`mɪt] (v.) 承認
11. **blessed** [`blesɪd] (a.) 受祝福的；快樂的

44

15

The sixth planet was ten times bigger than the last. It was inhabited by an old gentleman who wrote enormous[1] books.

"Ah, here comes an explorer[2]," he exclaimed when he caught sight of the little prince, who was feeling a little winded[3] and sat down on the desk. He had already traveled so much and so far!

"Where do you come from?" the old gentleman asked him.

"What's that big book?" asked the little prince. "What do you do with it?"

"I'm a geographer[4]," the old gentleman answered.

"And what's a geographer?"

"A scholar[5] who knows where the seas are, and the rivers, the cities, the mountains, and the deserts."

"That is very interesting," the little prince said. "Here at last is someone who has a real profession[6]!" And he gazed around[7] him at the geographer's planet. He had never seen a planet so majestic[8].

"Your planet is very beautiful," he said. "Does it have any oceans?"

"I couldn't say," said the geographer.

"Oh" The little prince was disappointed. "And mountains?"

"I couldn't say," said the geographer.

"And cities and rivers and deserts?"

"I couldn't tell you that, either," the geographer said.

---

1. **enormous** [ɪ`nɔ:rməs] (a.) 龐大的
2. **explorer** [ɪk`splɔ:rər] (n.) 探險者
3. **winded** [`wɪndɪd] (a.) 有風的
4. **geographer** [dʒi`ɑ:grəfər] (n.) 地理學家
5. **scholar** [`skɑ:lər] (n.) 學者
6. **profession** [prə`feʃən] (n.) 職業（尤指受過良好專門訓練的）（近似於 job, occupation)
7. **gaze around** 凝視於……
8. **majestic** [mə`dʒestɪk] (a.) 雄偉的

"But you're a geographer!"

"That's right," said the geographer, "but I'm not an explorer. There's not one explorer on my planet. A geographer doesn't go out to describe[1] cities, rivers, mountains, seas, oceans, and deserts. A geographer is too important to go wandering about[2]. He never leaves his study[3]. But he receives[4] the explorers there. He questions them, and he writes down what they remember. And if the memories of one of the explorers seem interesting to him, then the geographer conducts[5] an inquiry[6] into that explorer's moral[7] character[8]."

"Why is that?"

"Because an explorer who told lies would cause[9] disasters[10] in the geography books. As would an explorer who drank too much."

---

1. **describe** [dɪˋskraɪb] (v.) 描述；描繪
2. **wander about** 四處徘徊
3. **study** [ˋstʌdi] (n.) 研究；調查
4. **receive** [rɪˋsi:v] (v.) 接待；歡迎
5. **conduct** [kənˋdʌkt] (v.) 實施；處理
6. **inquiry** [ɪnˋkwaɪri] (n.) 探索；詢問

"Why is that?" the little prince asked again.

"Because drunkards see double. And the geographer would write down two mountains where there was only one."

---

7. **moral** [`mɔ:rəl]
   (a.) 道德上的
8. **character** [`kærɪktər]
   (n.) 人格特質
9. **cause** [kɑ:z]
   (v.) 引起；導致
10. **disaster** [dɪ`zæstər]
   (n.) 災害；災難

"I know someone," said the little prince, "who would be a bad explorer."

"Possibly. Well, when the explorer's moral character seems to be a good one, an investigation[1] is made into his discovery[2]."

"By going to see it?"

"No, that would be too complicated[3]. But the explorer is required[4] to furnish[5] proofs[6]. For instance, if he claims[7] to have discovered a large mountain, he is required to bring back[8] large stones from it." The geographer suddenly grew excited. "But you come from far away! You're an explorer! You must describe your planet for me!"

---

1. **investigation** [ɪnˌvestɪˋgeɪʃən] (n.) 探究；調查
2. **discovery** [dɪsˋkʌvəri] (n.) 發現
3. **complicated** [ˋkɑ:mplɪkeɪd] (a.) 複雜的；難懂的
4. **require** [rɪˋkwaɪr] (v.) 需要
5. **furnish** [ˋfɜ:rnɪʃ] (v.) 提供
6. **proof** [pru:f] (n.) 證據；物證
7. **claim** [kleɪm] (v.) 主張；聲稱
8. **bring back** 帶回

And the geographer, having opened his logbook[9], sharpened[10] his pencil. Explorers' reports are first recorded[11] in pencil; ink is used only after proofs have been furnished.

"Well?" said the geographer expectantly[12].

"Oh, where I live," said the little prince, "is not very interesting. It's so small. I have three volcanoes, two active and one extinct. But you never know."

"You never know," said the geographer.

"I also have a flower."

"We don't record flowers," the geographer said.

"Why not? It's the prettiest thing!"

"Because flowers are ephemeral[13]."

"What does *ephemeral* mean?"

9. **logbook** [ˋlɑ:gbuk] (n.) 旅行日誌
10. **sharpen** [ˋʃɑ:rpən] (v.) 削尖
11. **record** [rɪˋkɔ:rd] (v.) 記載；紀錄
12. **expectantly** [ɪkˋspektəntli] (adv.) 期待地；期望地
13. **ephemeral** [ɪˋfemərəl] (a.) 生命短暫的

47

"Geographies," said the geographer, "are the finest books of all. They never go out of fashion[1]. It is extremely[2] rare[3] for a mountain to change position[4]. It is extremely rare for an ocean to be drained[5] of its water. We write eternal[6] things."

"But extinct volcanoes can come back to life[7]," the little prince interrupted. "What does *ephemeral* mean?"

"Whether volcanoes are extinct or active comes down to[8] the same thing for us," said the geographer. "For us what counts[9] is the mountain. That doesn't change."

"But what does *ephemeral* mean?" repeated the little prince, who had never in all his life let go of a question once he had asked it.

---

1. **go out of fashion** 過時的
2. **extremely** [ɪk`stri:mli] (adv.) 極端地；非常地
3. **rare** [rer] (a.) 稀有的；罕見的
4. **position** [pə`zɪʃən] (n.) 位置；方位
5. **drain** [dreɪn] (v.) 流乾；枯竭
6. **eternal** [ɪ`tɜ:rnəl] (a.) 永恆的
7. **come back to life** 復活
8. **come down to** 到頭來
9. **count** [kaʊnt] (v.) 很重要；有價值
10. **threaten** [`θretn] (v.) 威脅

"It means, 'which is threatened[10] by imminent[11] disappearance[12].'"

"Is my flower threatened by imminent disappearance?"

"Of course."

"My flower is ephemeral," the little prince said to himself, "and she has only four thorns, with which to defend herself against the world! And I've left her all alone where I live!"

That was his first impulse[13] of regret. But he plucked up his courage[14] again. "Where would you advise me to visit?" he asked.

"The planet Earth," the geographer answered. "It has a good reputation[15]."

And the little prince went on his way, thinking about his flower.

---

11. **imminent** [`ɪmənənt] (a.) 即將發生的
12. **disappearance** [ˏdɪsə`pɪrəns] (n.) 消失；滅絕
13. **impulse** [`ɪmpʌls] (n.) 衝動；一時的念頭
14. **pluck up one's courage** 鼓起……勇氣
15. **reputation** [ˏrepju`teɪʃən] (n.) 聲譽

48

16

The seventh planet, then, was the Earth. The Earth is not just another planet! It contains[1] one hundred and eleven kings (including, of course, the African kings), seven thousand geographers, nine hundred thousand businessmen, seven-and-a-half million drunkards, three-hundred-eleven million vain men; in other words, about two billion grown-ups.

To give you a notion[2] of the Earth's dimensions[3], I can tell you that before the invention of electricity, it was necessary to maintain[4], over the whole of six continents[5], a veritable[6] army of[7] four-hundred-sixty-two thousand, five hundred and eleven lamplighters.

---

1. **contain** [kən`teɪn] (v.) 包含
2. **notion** [`noʊʃən] (n.) 概念
3. **dimension** [daɪ`menʃən] (n.) 尺寸；大小
4. **maintain** [meɪn`teɪn] (v.) 保持；維持
5. **continent** [`kɑ:ntənənt] (n.) 大洲；大陸
6. **veritable** [`verɪtəbəl] (a.) 名副其實的
7. **an army of** 大群；大批
8. **splendid** [`splendɪd] (a.) 有光彩的；燦爛的
9. **ordered** [`ɔ:rdərd] (a.) 有紀律的；有條理的
10. **ballet** [`bæle] (n.) 芭蕾

Seen from some distance, this made a splendid[8] effect. The movements of this army were ordered[9] like those of a ballet[10].

First came the turn of the lamplighters of New Zealand and Australia; then these, having lit their street lamps, would go home to sleep.

Next it would be the turn of the lamplighters of China and Siberia to perform their steps in the lamplighters' ballet, and then they too would vanish[11] into the wings[12].

Then came the turn of the lamplighters of Russia and India. Then those of Africa and Europe. Then those of South America, and of North America. And they never missed their cues[13] for their appearances onstage[14]. It was awe-inspiring[15].

Only the lamplighter of the single street lamp at the North Pole and his colleague[16] of the single street lamp at the South Pole led[17] carefree[18], idle[19] lives: They worked twice a year.

---

11. **vanish** [`vænɪʃ] (v.) 消失
12. **wing** [wɪŋ] (n.) 舞台側面
13. **miss one's cue** 錯失……的角色
14. **onstage** [ɑ:n`steɪdʒ] (a.) 在舞台上演出的
15. **awe-inspiring** 令人驚嘆的
16. **colleague** [`kɑ:li:g] (n.) 同伴；同僚
17. **lead** [li:d] (v.) 過（活）
18. **carefree** [`kerfri:] (a.) 輕鬆愉快的；無憂無慮的
19. **idle** [`aɪdl] (a.) 不工作的；悠閒的

49

17

Trying to be witty[1] leads to lying, more or less. What I just told you about the lamplighters isn't completely true, and I risk[2] giving a false idea of our planet to those who don't know it. Men occupy[3] very little space on Earth. If the two billion inhabitants of the globe[4] were to stand close together, as they might for some big public event, they would easily fit into[5] a city block that was twenty miles long and twenty miles wide. You could crowd[6] all humanity[7] onto the smallest Pacific[8] islet[9].

---

1. **witty** [ˋwɪti] (a.) 機智的
2. **risk** [rɪsk] (v.) 冒……的風險
3. **occupy** [ˋɑ:kjupaɪ] (v.) 佔領；佔據
4. **globe** [gloʊb] (n.) 地球；球狀物
5. **fit into** 適應於……
6. **crowd** [kraʊd] (v.) 聚集
7. **humanity** [hju:ˋmænəti] (n.) 人類
8. **Pacific** [pəˋsɪfɪk] (n.) 太平洋
9. **islet** [ˋaɪlɪt] (n.) 小島

The little prince was quite surprised not to see anyone.

50

Grown-ups, of course, won't believe you. They're convinced[1] they take up[2] much more room. They consider[3] themselves as important as the baobabs.

So you should advise them to make their own calculations — they love numbers, and they'll enjoy it. But don't waste your time on this extra[4] task. It's unnecessary. Trust me.

So once he reached Earth, the little prince was quite surprised not to see anyone. He was beginning to fear he had come to the wrong planet, when a moon-colored loop[5] uncoiled[6] on the sand.

"Good evening," the little prince said, just in case[7].

"Good evening," said the snake.

"What planet have I landed on[8]?" asked the little prince.

---

1. **convinced** [kən`vɪnst] (a.) 確信的
2. **take up** 佔去
3. **consider** [kən`sɪdər] (v.) 認為；視為

"On the planet Earth, in Africa," the snake replied.

"Ah! . . . And are there no people on Earth?"

"It's the desert here. There are no people in the desert. Earth is very big," said the snake.

The little prince sat down on a rock and looked up into the sky.

"I wonder[9]," he said, "if the stars are lit up so that each of us can find his own, someday. Look at my planet — it's just overhead[10]. But so far away!"

"It's lovely," the snake said. "What have you come to Earth for?"

"I'm having difficulties with a flower," the little prince said.

"Ah!" said the snake.

And they were both silent.

---

4. **extra** [`ekstrə] (a.) 額外的；另外的
5. **loop** [lu:p] (n.) 圈；環
6. **uncoil** [ʌn`kɔɪl] (v.) 展開；解開
7. **just in case** 只是以防萬一
8. **land on** 登陸
9. **wonder** [`wʌndər] (v.) 納悶；懷疑
10. **overhead** [`ouvər`hed] (a.) 在頭頂上的

"You're a funny creature, no thicker than a finger."

"Where are the people?" The little prince finally resumed[1] the conversation[2]. "It's a little lonely in the desert . . ."

"It's also lonely with people," said the snake.

The little prince looked at the snake for a long time. "You're a funny creature[3]," he said at last, "no thicker[4] than a finger."

"But I'm more powerful than a king's finger," the snake said.

The little prince smiled.

"You're not very powerful . . . You don't even have feet. You couldn't travel very far."

"I can take you further[5] than a ship," the snake said. He coiled[6] around the little prince's ankle[7], like a golden bracelet[8].

---

1. **resume** [rɪ`zu:m] (v.) 重新開始
2. **conversation** [ˌkɑ:nvər`seɪʃən] (n.) 會話；談話
3. **creature** [`kri:tʃər] (n.) 傢伙；生物
4. **thick** [θɪk] (a.) 厚的
5. **further** [`fɜ:rðər] (a.) （**far** 的比較級）更遠的
6. **coil** [kɔɪl] (v.) 捲；盤繞
7. **ankle** [`æŋkəl] (n.) 足踝
8. **bracelet** [`breɪslɪt] (n.) 手環

52

"Anyone I touch, I send back to the land from which he came," the snake went on. "But you're innocent, and you come from a star . . ."

The little prince made no reply.

"I feel sorry for you, being so weak on this granite[1] earth," said the snake. "I can help you, someday, if you grow too homesick[2] for your planet. I can—"

"Oh, I understand just what you mean," said the little prince, "but why do you always speak in riddles[3]?"

"I solve them all," said the snake.

And they were both silent.

---

1. **granite** [`grænɪt] (n.) 花崗岩
2. **homesick** [`hoʊmsɪk] (a.) 思鄉的
3. **speak in riddles** 打謎似的說
4. **encounter** [ɪn`kaʊntər] (v.) 偶遇
5. **petal** [`petl] (n.) 花瓣
6. **consequence** [`kɑ:nsɪˏkwens] (n.) 自大；神氣活現
   of no consequence 無足輕重
7. **inquire** [ɪn`kwaɪr] (v.) 詢問
8. **caravan** [`kærəvæn] (n.)（來往於沙漠的）商隊
9. **root** [ru:t] (n.) 根（此引申為家）
10. **hamper** [`hæmpər] (v.) 束縛；妨礙
11. **a good deal** 許多；非常

18

The little prince crossed the desert and encountered[4] only one flower. A flower with three petals[5] — a flower of no consequence[6]. . .

"Good morning," said the little prince.

"Good morning," said the flower.

"Where are the people?" the little prince inquired[7] politely.

The flower had one day seen a caravan[8] passing.

"People? There are six or seven of them, I believe, in existence. I caught sight of them years ago. But you never know where to find them. The wind blows them away. They have no roots[9], which hampers[10] them a good deal[11]."

"Good-bye," said the little prince.

"Good-bye," said the flower.

53

19

The little prince climbed a high mountain. The only mountains he had ever known were the three volcanoes, which came up to his knee[1]. And he used the extinct volcano as a footstool[2]. "From a mountain as high as this one," he said to himself, "I'll get a view of the whole planet and all the people on it . . ." But he saw nothing but rocky[3] peaks[4] as sharp as needles[5].

"Hello," he said, just in case.

"Hello . . . hello . . . hello . . . ," the echo[6] answered.

"Who are you?" asked the little prince.

"Who are you. . . who are you . . . who are you . . . ," the echo answered.

---

1. **knee** [ni:] (n.) 膝蓋
2. **footstool** [ˋfʊtstu:l] (n.) 腳凳
3. **rocky** [ˋrɑ:ki] (a.) 岩石構成的
4. **peak** [pi:k] (n.) 山峰
5. **needle** [ˋni:dl] (n.) 針
6. **echo** [ˋekoʊ] (n.) 回聲；回音
7. **peculiar** [pɪˋkju:liər] (a.) 奇怪的；罕見的
8. **imagination** [ɪˏmædʒɪˋneɪʃən] (n.) 想像力；創造力

"Let's be friends. I'm lonely," he said.

"I'm lonely . . . I'm lonely . . . I'm lonely . . . ," the echo answered.

"What a peculiar[7] planet!" he thought. "It's all dry and sharp and hard. And people here have no imagination[8]. They repeat whatever you say to them. Where I live I had a flower: She always spoke first . . ."

What a peculiar planet!
It's all dry and sharp and hard.

20

54

But it so happened that the little prince, having walked a long time through sand and rocks and snow, finally discovered a road. And all roads go to where there are people.

"Good morning," he said.

It was a blossoming[1] rose garden.

"Good morning," said the roses.

The little prince gazed[2] at them. All of them looked like his flower.

"Who are you?" he asked, astounded[3].

"We're roses," the roses said.

"Ah!" said the little prince.

And he felt very unhappy. His flower had told him she was the only one of her kind in the whole universe. And here were five thousand of them, all just alike[4], in just one garden!

"She would be very annoyed[5]," he said to himself, "if she saw this . . . She would cough terribly and pretend[6] to be dying, to avoid[7] being laughed at. And I'd have to pretend to be nursing[8] her; otherwise[9], she'd really let herself die in order to humiliate[10] me."

---

1. **blossom** [`blɑ:səm]
   (v.) 生長茂盛
2. **gaze** [geɪz] (v.)
   凝視；注視
3. **astounded** [ə`staʊndɪd]
   (a.) 被震驚的；受驚嚇的
4. **alike** [ə`laɪk] (a.)
   相像的；相同的
5. **annoyed** [ə`nɔɪd] (a.)
   惱怒的；氣惱的
6. **pretend** [prɪ`tend]
   (v.) 假裝；佯裝
7. **avoid** [ə`vɔɪd] (v.)
   避開；躲開
8. **nurse** [nɜ:rs] (v.)
   照顧；細心照料
9. **otherwise** [`ʌðərwaɪz]
   (adv.) 否則；不然
10. **humiliate** [hju:`mɪlieɪt]
   (v.) 使丟臉；使蒙羞

55

And then he said to himself, "I thought I was rich because I had just one flower, and all I own is an ordinary[1] rose. That and my three volcanoes, which come up to my knee, one of which may be permanently[2] extinct. It doesn't make me much of a prince. . ." And he lay down in the grass and wept[3].

And he lay down in the grass and wept.

21

It was then that the fox appeared.

"Good morning," said the fox.

"Good morning," the little prince answered politely[4], though when he turned around he saw nothing.

"I'm here," the voice said, "under the apple tree."

"Who are you?" the little prince asked. "You're very pretty . . ."

"I'm a fox," the fox said.

"Come and play with me," the little prince proposed[5]. "I'm feeling so sad."

"I can't play with you," the fox said. "I'm not tamed[6]."

"Ah! Excuse me," said the little prince. But upon reflection[7] he added, "What does *tamed* mean?"

---

1. **ordinary** [`ɔ:rdəneri] (a.) 普通的；平常的
2. **permanently** [`pɜ:rmənəntli] (adv.) 長期不變地；永久地
3. **weep** [wi:p] (v.) 哭泣；流淚 (weep-wept-wept)
4. **politely** [pə`laɪtli] (adv.) 有禮貌地
5. **propose** [prə`pouz] (v.) 提出；建議
6. **tame** [teɪm] (v.) 馴養；馴化
7. **upon reflection** 在思考之後

56

"You're not from around here," the fox said. "What are you looking for[1]?"

"I'm looking for people," said the little prince. "What does *tamed* mean?"

"People," said the fox, "have guns[2] and they hunt[3]. It's quite troublesome[4]. And they also raise[5] chickens. That's the only interesting thing about them. Are you looking for chickens?"

"No," said the little prince, "I'm looking for friends. What does *tamed* mean?"

"It's something that's been too often neglected[6]. It means, 'to create ties'. . ."

"To create ties[7]?"

"That's right." the fox said. "For me you're only a little boy just like a hundred thousand other little boys. And I have no need of you. And you have no need of me, either. For you I'm only a fox like a hundred thousand other foxes. But if you tame me, we'll need each other. You'll be the only boy in the world for me. I'll be the only fox in the world for you . . ."

---

1. **look for** 尋找
2. **gun** [gʌn] (n.) 槍
3. **hunt** [hʌnt] (v.) 打獵；獵捕
4. **troublesome** [ˋtrʌbəlsəm] (a.) 令人煩惱的；討厭的
5. **raise** [reɪz] (v.) 飼養；養育
6. **neglect** [nɪˋglekt] (v.) 忽略；疏漏
7. **tie** [taɪ] (n.) 聯繫

57

"I'm beginning to understand," the little prince said. "There's a flower . . . I think she's tamed me . . ."

"Possibly," the fox said. "On Earth, one sees all kinds of things."

"Oh, this isn't on Earth," the little prince said.

The fox seemed quite intrigued[1]. "On another planet?"

"Yes."

"Are there hunters on that planet?"

"No."

"Now that's interesting. And chickens?"

"No."

"Nothing's perfect," sighed the fox.

But he returned to his idea. "My life is monotonous[2]. I hunt chickens; people hunt me. All chickens are just alike, and all men are just alike. So I'm rather[3] bored. But if you tame me, my life will be filled with[4] sunshine. I'll know the sound of footsteps[5] that will be different from all the rest. Other footsteps send me back underground. Yours will call me out of my burrow[6] like music.

And then, look! You see the wheat fields over there? I don't eat bread. For me wheat is of no use[7] whatever[8]. Wheat fields say nothing to me. Which is sad. But you have hair the color of gold. So it will be wonderful, once you've tamed me! The wheat[9], which is golden, will remind me of you[10]. And I'll love the sound of the wind in the wheat . . ."

---

1. **intrigued** [ɪn`tri:gd] (a.) 好奇的；迷住了的
2. **monotonous** [mə`nɑ:tənəs] (a.) 單調的；無聊的
3. **rather** [`ræðər] (adv.) 相當；有點兒
4. **be filled with** 充滿
5. **footstep** [`futstep] (n.) 腳步；步伐
6. **burrow** [`bɜ:roʊ] (n.) (兔、狐) 穴；地道
7. **be of no use** 沒有用處
8. **whatever** [wa:t`ever] (adv.) 無論如何
9. **wheat** [wi:t] (n.) 小麥
10. **remind A of B** 使 A 想起 B

58

The fox fell silent and stared at the little prince for a long while. "Please . . . tame me!" he said.

"I'd like to," the little prince replied, "but I haven't much time. I have friends to find and so many things to learn."

"The only things you learn are the things you tame," said the fox. "People haven't time to learn anything. They buy things ready-made[1] in stores. But since there are no stores where you can buy friends, people no longer have friends. If you want a friend, tame me!"

"What do I have to do?" asked the little prince.

1. **ready-make** 製作完成的；現成的
2. **patient** [ˋpeɪʃənt] (a.) 有耐心的
3. **watch out of the corner of one's eyes** 瞥見
4. **source** [sɔːrs] (n.) 來源

"You have to be very patient[2]," the fox answered. "First you'll sit down a little ways away from me, over there, in the grass. I'll watch you out of the corner of my eye[3], and you won't say anything. Language is the source[4] of misunderstandings[5]. But day by day[6], you'll be able to sit a little closer . . ."

The next day the little prince returned.

"It would have been better to return at the same time," the fox said. "For instance, if you come at four in the afternoon, I'll begin to be happy by three.

The closer it gets to four, the happier I'll feel. By four I'll be all excited and worried; I'll discover what it costs[7] to be happy! But if you come at any time, I'll never know when I should prepare my heart . . . There must be rites[8]."

"What's a *rite* ?" asked the little prince.

---

5. **misunderstanding** [ˏmɪsʌndər`stændɪŋ] (n.) 誤解
6. **day by day** 一天天
7. **cost** [kɑːst] (v.) 付出；花費 (cost-cost-cost)
8. **rite** [raɪt] (n.) 慣例

"If you come at four in the afternoon, I'll begin to be happy by three."

"That's another thing that's been too often neglected," said the fox. "It's the fact that one day is different from the other days, one hour from the other hours. My hunters, for example, have a rite. They dance with the village girls on Thursdays.

So Thursday's a wonderful day: I can take a stroll[1] all the way to[2] the vineyards[3]. If the hunters danced whenever they chose, the days would all be just alike, and I'd have no holiday at all."

That was how the little prince tamed the fox. And when the time to leave was near:

"Ah!" the fox said. "I shall weep."

"It's your own fault," the little prince said. "I never wanted to do you any harm[4], but you insisted[5] that I tame you . . ."

"Yes, of course," the fox said.

---

1. **take a stroll** 散步；閒逛
2. **all the way to** 一路至……
3. **vineyard** [`vɪnjərd] (n.) 葡萄園
4. **do A harm** 傷害 A
5. **insist** [ɪn`sɪst] (v.) 堅持

"But you're going to weep[1]!" said the little prince.

"Yes, of course," the fox said.

"Then you get nothing out of it?"

"I get something," the fox said, "because of the color of the wheat." Then he added, "Go look at the roses again. You'll understand that yours is the only rose in all the world. Then come back to say good-bye, and I'll make you the gift of a secret."

The little prince went to look at the roses again.

"You're not at all like my rose. You're nothing at all yet," he told them. "No one has tamed you and you haven't tamed anyone. You're the way my fox was. He was just a fox like a hundred thousand others. But I've made him my friend, and now he's the only fox in all the world."

And the roses were humbled[2].

---

1. **weep** [wi:p] (v.) 流淚
2. **humble** [`hʌmbl] (v.) 使……感到不如人
3. **ordinary** [`ɔ:rdəneri] (a.) 平常的；普通的
4. **passerby** [`pæsər`baɪ] (n.) 路人；過客
5. **shelter** [`ʃeltər] (v.) 保護；遮蔽
6. **complain** [kəm`pleɪn] (v.) 抱怨；發牢騷
7. **boast** [boust] (v.) 誇耀；吹噓
8. **essential** [ɪ`sentʃəl] (a.) 必要的；精華的
9. **invisible** [ɪn`vɪzɪbəl] (a.) 看不見的

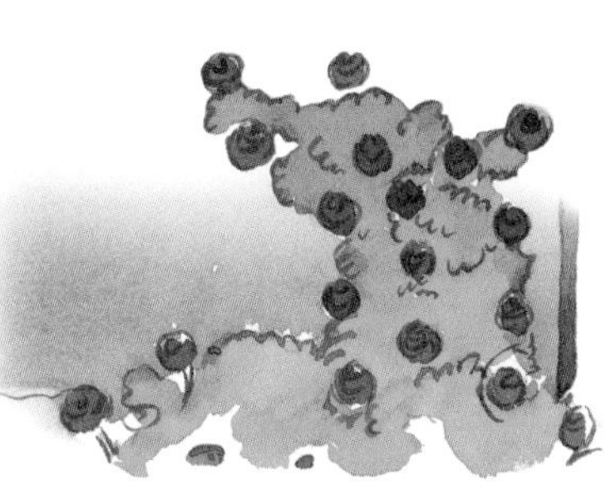

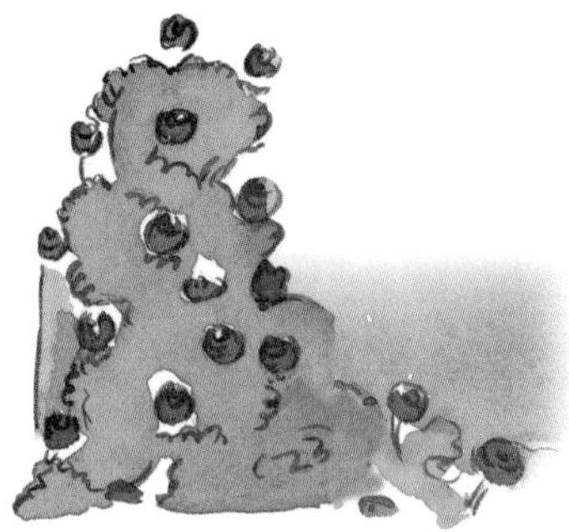

"You are lovely, but you're empty," he went on. "One couldn't die for you. Of course, an ordinary[3] passerby[4] would think my rose looked just like you. But my rose, all on her own, is more important than all of you together, since she's the one I've watered. Since she's the one I put under glass. Since she's the one I sheltered[5] behind a screen. Since she's the one for whom I killed the caterpillars (except the two or three for butterflies). Since she's the one I listened to when she complained[6], or when she boasted[7], or even sometimes when she said nothing at all. Since she's *my* rose."

And he went back to the fox.

"Good-bye," he said.

"Good-bye," said the fox. "Here is my secret. It's quite simple: One sees clearly only with the heart. Anything essential[8] is invisible[9] to the eyes."

61

"Anything essential is invisible to the eyes," the little prince repeated, in order to remember.

"It's the time you spent on your rose that makes your rose so important."

"It's the time I spent on my rose. . . ," the little prince repeated, in order to remember.

"People have forgotten this truth," the fox said. "But you mustn't forget it. You become responsible[1] forever for what you've tamed. You're responsible for your rose . . ."

"I'm responsible for my rose . . . ," the little prince repeated, in order to remember.

---

1. **responsible** [rɪ`spɑ:nsəbəl] (a.) 負責的
2. **switchman** [`swɪtʃmæn] (n.)（鐵路的）扳道工
3. **sort** [sɔ:rt] (v.) 把……分類
4. **bundle** [`bʌndl] (n.) 捆；束
5. **dispatch** [dɪ`spætʃ] (v.) 分派
6. **roar** [rɔ:r] (v.) 呼嘯
7. **cabin** [`kæbɪn] (n.) 小屋
8. **locomotive** [ˌloukə`moutɪv] (n.) 火車頭
9. **thunder** [`θʌndər] (v.) 轟隆隆地移動

22

"Good morning," said the little prince.

"Good morning," said the railway switchman[2].

"What is it that you do here?" asked the little prince.

"I sort[3] the travelers into bundles[4] of a thousand," the switchman said. "I dispatch[5] the trains that carry them, sometimes to the right, sometimes to the left."

And a brightly lit express train, roaring[6] like thunder, shook the switchman's cabin[7].

"What a hurry they're in," said the little prince. "What are they looking for?"

"Not even the engineer on the locomotive[8] knows," the switchman said.

And another brightly lit express train thundered[9] by in the opposite direction.

"Are they coming back already?" asked the little prince.

"It's not the same ones," the switchman said. "It's an exchange."

"They weren't satisfied, where they were?" asked the little prince.

"No one is ever satisfied where he is," the switchman said.

And a third brightly lit express train thundered past.

"Are they chasing[1] the first travelers?" asked the little prince.

"They're not chasing anything," the switchman said. "They're sleeping in there, or else they're yawning. Only the children are pressing their noses against the windowpanes[2]."

"Only the children know what they're looking for," said the little prince. "They spend their time on a rag doll[3] and it becomes very important, and if it's taken away from[4] them, they cry . . ."

"They're lucky," the switchman said.

1. **chase** [tʃeɪs] (v.) 追逐；追趕
2. **windowpane** [`wɪndoupeɪn] (n.) 玻璃窗
3. **rag doll** 布洋娃娃
4. **take away from** 從……身邊奪走
5. **pill** [pɪl] (n.) 藥丸；藥片

23

"Good morning," said the little prince.

"Good morning," said the salesclerk. This was a salesclerk who sold pills[5] invented to quench[6] thirst[7]. Swallow one a week and you no longer feel any need to drink.

"Why do you sell these pills?"

"They save so much time," the salesclerk said. "Experts[8] have calculated that you can save fifty-three minutes a week."

"And what do you do with those fifty-three minutes?"

"Whatever you like."

"If I had fifty-three minutes to spend as I liked," the little prince said to himself, "I'd walk very slowly toward a water fountain[9]. . ."

---

6. **quench** [kwentʃ] (v.) 解（渴）；抑制
7. **thirst** [θɜːrst] (n.) 口渴
8. **expert** [`ekspɜːrt] (n.) 專家
9. **fountain** [`faʊntn] (n.) 噴泉；泉水

24

It was now the eighth day since my crash landing in the desert, and I'd listened to the story about the salesclerk as I was drinking the last drop[1] of my water supply[2].

"Ah," I said to the little prince, "your memories are very pleasant[3], but I haven't yet repaired my plane. I have nothing left to drink, and I, too, would be glad to walk very slowly toward a water fountain!"

"My friend the fox told me —"

"Little fellow, this has nothing to do with[4] the fox!"

"Why?"

"Because we're going to die of thirst."

The little prince didn't follow[5] my reasoning[6], and answered me, "It's good to have had a friend, even if you're going to die. Myself, I'm very glad to have had a fox for a friend."

"He doesn't realize the danger[7]," I said to myself. "He's never hungry or thirsty. A little sunlight is enough for him . . ."

But the little prince looked at me and answered my thought. "I'm thirsty, too . . . Let's find a well[8] . . ."

I made an exasperated[9] gesture. It is absurd looking for a well, at random[10], in the vastness[11] of the desert. But even so, we started walking.

---

1. **drop** [drɑ:p] (n.) (一) 滴
2. **supply** [sə`plaɪ] (v.) 供給；供應
3. **pleasant** [`plezənt] (a.) 令人愉快的
4. **have nothing to do with** 與……無關
5. **follow** [`fɑ:loʊ] (v.) 跟隨
6. **reasoning** [`ri:zənɪŋ] (n.) 推論；理由
7. **danger** [`deɪndʒər] (n.) 危險
8. **well** [wel] (n.) 水井；井
9. **exasperate** [ɪg`zæspəreɪt] (v.) 使惱怒
10. **at random** 隨便地；任意地
11. **vastness** [`væstnɪs] (n.) 龐大；巨大

64

When we had walked for several hours in silence, night fell and stars began to appear. I noticed[1] them as in a dream, being somewhat[2] feverish[3] on account of[4] my thirst. The little prince's words danced in my memory.

"So you're thirsty, too?" I asked.

But he didn't answer my question.

He merely[5] said to me, "Water can also be good for the heart . . ."

I didn't understand his answer, but I said nothing . . . I knew by this time[6] that it was no use questioning him.

He was tired. He sat down. I sat down next to him. And after a silence, he spoke again. "The stars are beautiful because of a flower you don't see . . ."

I answered, "Yes, of course," and without speaking another word I stared at the ridges[7] of sand in the moonlight.

"The desert is beautiful," the little prince added.

And it was true. I've always loved the desert. You sit down on a sand dune[8]. You see nothing. You hear nothing. And yet something shines, something sings in that silence . . . .

"What makes the desert beautiful," the little prince said, "is that it hides a well somewhere . . ."

I was surprised by suddenly understanding that mysterious radiance[9] of the sands. When I was a little boy I lived in an old house, and there was a legend[10] that a treasure was buried in it somewhere.

---

1. **notice** [`noutɪs] (v.) 注意；注意到
2. **somewhat** [`sʌmwɑ:t] (adv.) 稍微；有點
3. **feverish** [`fi:vərɪʃ] (a.) 發熱的；發燒的
4. **on account of** 因為；由於
5. **merely** [`mɪrli] (adv.) 僅僅；只是
6. **by this time** 到了這時
7. **ridge** [rɪdʒ] (n.) 背脊
8. **dune** [du:n] (n.) 沙丘
9. **radiance** [`reɪdiəns] (n.) 發光；光輝
10. **legend** [`ledʒənd] (n.) 傳說

65

Of course, no one was ever able to find the treasure, perhaps no one even searched. But it cast a spell over[1] that whole house. My house hid a secret in the depths of[2] its heart . . . .

"Yes," I said to the little prince, "whether it's a house or the stars or the desert, what makes them beautiful is invisible!"

"I'm glad," he said, "you agree with my fox."

As the little prince was falling asleep, I picked him up in my arms, and started walking again. I was moved[3].

It was as if I was carrying a fragile[4] treasure. It actually seemed to me there was nothing more fragile on Earth.

By the light of the moon, I gazed at that pale[5] forehead[6], those closed eyes, those locks[7] of hair trembling[8] in the wind, and I said to myself, "What I'm looking at is only a shell. What's most important is invisible . . ."

---

1. **cast a spell over** 向……施魔法
2. **in the depths of** 在……深處
3. **be moved** 被感動
4. **fragile** [ˋfrædʒəl] (a.) 易碎的
5. **pale** [peɪl] (a.) 蒼白的
6. **forehead** [ˋfɔ:rhed] (n.) 額頭
7. **lock** [lɑ:k] (n.) 一綹頭髮
8. **tremble** [ˋtrembəl] (v.) 震顫；抖動
9. **part** [pɑ:rt] (v.) 分開

As his lips parted[9] in a half smile, I said to myself, again, "What moves me so deeply about this sleeping little prince is his loyalty[10] to a flower — the image of a rose shining within him like the flame[11] within a lamp, even when he's asleep . . ." And I realized he was even more fragile than I had thought. Lamps must be protected: A gust[12] of wind can blow them out[13]. . . .

And walking on like that, I found the well at daybreak[14].

---

10. **loyalty** [`lɔɪəlti] (n.) 忠誠；忠心
11. **flame** [fleɪm] (n.) 火焰；光芒
12. **gust** [gʌst] (n.) 一陣強風
13. **blow out** 吹熄；吹滅
14. **daybreak** [`deɪbreɪk] (n.) 黎明；破曉 (= dawn)

25

The little prince said, "People start out in express[1] trains, but they no longer know what they're looking for. Then they get all excited and rush around in circles . . ." And he added, "It's not worth the trouble[2] . . ."

The well we had come to was not at all like the wells of the Sahara. The wells of the Sahara are no more than holes[3] dug[4] in the sand. This one looked more like a village well. But there was no village here, and I thought I was dreaming.

"It's strange," I said to the little prince, "everything is ready: the pulley[5], the bucket, and the rope . . ."

He laughed, grasped[6] the rope, and set the pulley working. And the pulley groaned[7] the way an old weather vane[8] groans when the wind has been asleep a long time.

1. **express** [ɪk`spres] (n.) 快(車);直達快車
2. **worth the trouble** 值得費心
3. **hole** [hoʊl] (n.) 洞穴
4. **dig** [dɪg] (v.) 挖;掘 (dig-dug-dug)
5. **pulley** [`pʊli] (n.) 滑輪
6. **grasp** [græsp] (v.) 抓住
7. **groan** [groʊn] (v.) 呻吟
8. **weather vane** 風標;風向計

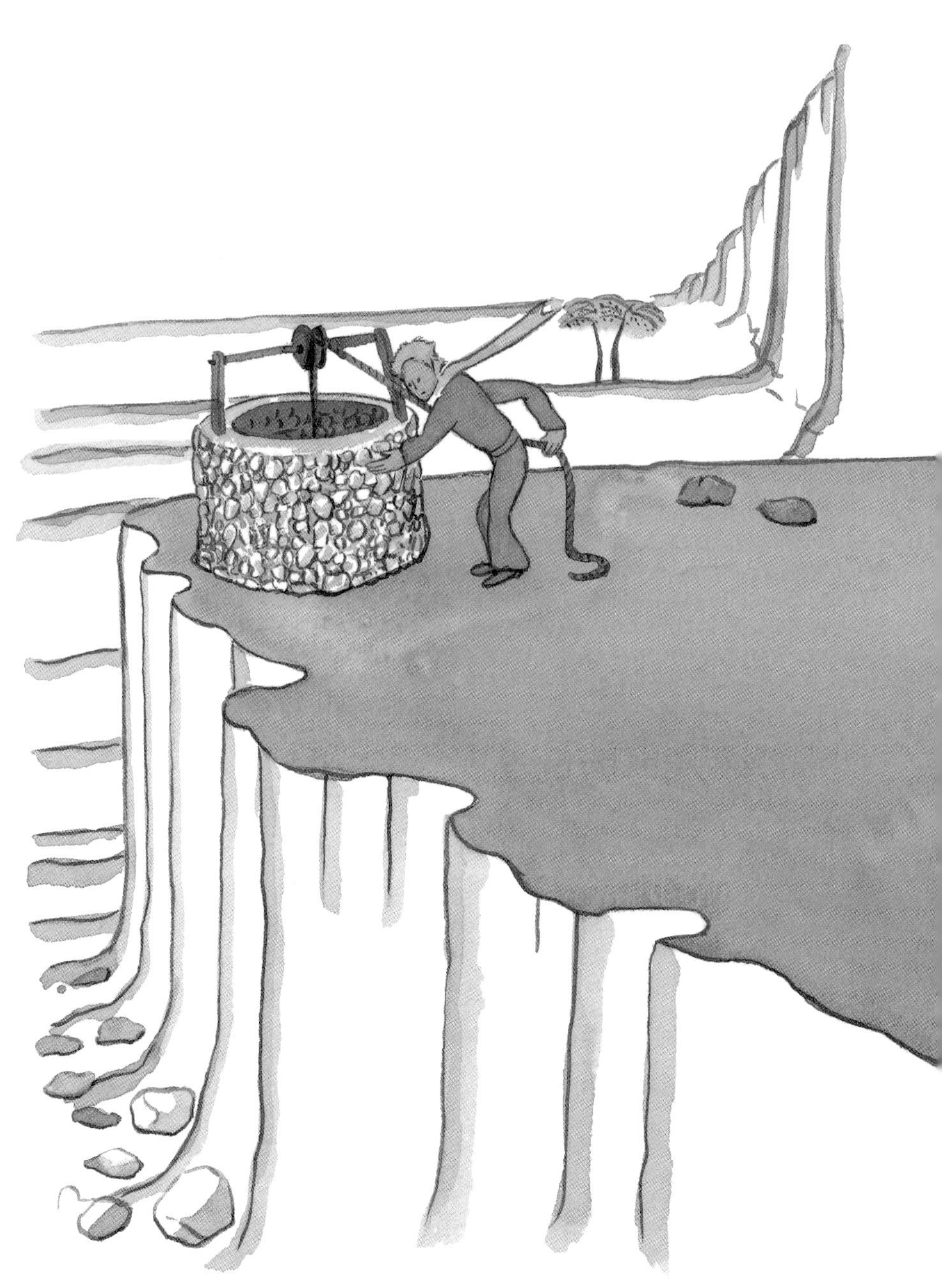

He laughed, grasped the rope, and set the pulley working.

67

"Hear that?" said the little prince. "We've awakened[1] this well and it's singing."

I didn't want him to tire himself out[2]. "Let me do that," I said to him. "It's too heavy for you."

Slowly I hoisted[3] the bucket to the edge[4] of the well. I set it down with great care. The song of the pulley continued in my ears, and I saw the sun glisten[5] on the still-trembling[6] water.

"I'm thirsty for that water," said the little prince. "Let me drink some . . ."

And I understood what he'd been looking for!

I raised the bucket to his lips. He drank, eyes closed. It was as sweet as a feast[7]. That water was more than merely[8] a drink.

It was born of[9] our walk beneath the stars, of the song of the pulley, of the effort of my arms. It did the heart good, like a present. When I was a little boy, the Christmas-tree lights, the music of midnight mass[10], the tenderness of people's smiles made up, in the same way, the whole radiance of the Christmas present I received.

"People where you live," the little prince said, "grow five thousand roses in one garden . . . yet[11] they don't find what they're looking for . . ."

"They don't find it," I answered.

"And yet what they're looking for could be found in a single rose, or a little water . . ."

"Of course," I answered.

And the little prince added, "But eyes are blind[12]. You have to look with the heart."

---

1. **awaken** [ə`weɪkən] (v.) 喚醒
2. **tire out** 使累垮
3. **hoist** [hɔɪst] (v.) 升起；吊起
4. **edge** [edʒ] (n.) 邊緣
5. **glisten** [`glɪsən] (v.) 閃耀
6. **still-trembling** 依然抖動的
7. **feast** [fi:st] (n.) 大餐；盛宴
8. **merely** [`mɪrli] (adv.) 僅僅；只是
9. **be born of** 出自於……；基於……
10. **mass** [mæs] (n.) 彌撒儀式
11. **yet** [jet] (conj.) 可是；然而
12. **blind** [blaɪnd] (a.) 瞎的；盲的

68

I had drunk the water. I could breathe[1] easy now. The sand, at daybreak, is honey colored. And that color was making me happy, too. Why then did I also feel so sad?

"You must keep your promise[2]," said the little prince, sitting up again beside me.

"What promise?"

"You know . . . a muzzle[3] for my sheep . . . I'm responsible for this flower!"

I took my drawings out of my pocket. The little prince glanced at them and laughed as he said, "Your baobabs look more like cabbages[4]."

"Oh!" I had been so proud of the baobabs!

"Your fox . . . his ears . . . look more like horns[5]. . . and they're too long!" And he laughed again.

"You're being unfair[6], my little prince," I said. "I never knew how to draw anything but boas from the inside and boas from the outside."

---

1. **breathe** [bri:ð] (v.) 呼吸
2. **keep one's promise** 實踐……的諾言
3. **muzzle** [`mʌzəl] (n.)（動物的）口套
4. **cabbage** [`kæbɪdʒ] (n.) 甘藍菜；捲心菜
5. **horn** [hɔ:rn] (n.) 角
6. **unfair** [ʌn`fer] (a.) 不公平的

"Oh, that'll be all right," he said. "Children understand."

So then I drew a muzzle. And with a heavy heart I handed[7] it to him. "You've made plans I don't know about . . ."

But he didn't answer. He said, "You know, my fall to Earth . . . Tomorrow will be the first anniversary[8] . . ." Then, after a silence, he continued. "I landed very near here . . ." And he blushed[9].

And once again, without understanding why, I felt a strange grief[10]. However, a question occurred[11] to me: "Then it wasn't by accident[12] that on the morning I met you, eight days ago, you were walking that way, all alone, a thousand miles from any inhabited region? Were you returning to the place where you fell to Earth?"

---

7. **hand** [hænd] (v.) 親手交給
8. **anniversary** [ˌænɪˋvɜːrsəri] (n.) 週年紀念日
9. **blush** [blʌʃ] (v.) 臉紅
10. **grief** [griːf] (n.) 悲傷；悲痛
11. **occur** [əˋkɜːr] (v.) 被想起；浮現
12. **by accident** 偶然地；意外地

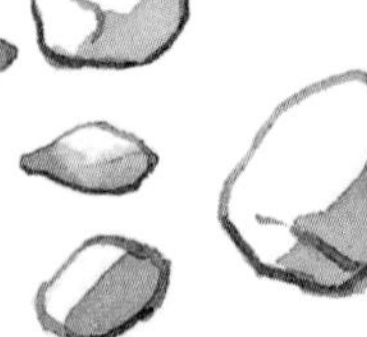

The little prince blushed again.

And I added, hesitantly[1], "Perhaps on account . . . of the anniversary?"

The little prince blushed once more. He never answered questions, but when someone blushes, doesn't that mean "yes"?

"Ah," I said to the little prince, "I'm afraid . . ."

But he answered, "You must get to work now. You must get back to your engine. I'll wait here. Come back tomorrow night."

But I wasn't reassured[2]. I remembered the fox. You risk[3] tears if you let yourself be tamed.

---

1. **hesitantly** [ˋhezətəntli] (adv.) 遲疑地
2. **reassure** [ˏriːəˋʃʊr] (v.) 再保證；使放心
3. **risk** [rɪsk] (v.) 冒……的風險
4. **ruin** [ˋruːɪn] (n.) 廢墟
5. **from a distance** 遠遠地
6. **dangle** [ˋdæŋgəl] (v.) 懸擺
7. **track** [træk] (n.) 足跡；行蹤
8. **yard** [jɑːrd] (n.) 碼（=0.91 公尺）
9. **poison** [ˋpɔɪzən] (n.) 毒物
10. **suffer** [ˋsʌfər] (v.) 受苦
11. **pound** [paʊnd] (v.) （心）劇跳

26

Beside the well, there was a ruin[4], an old stone wall. When I came back from my work the next evening, I caught sight of my little prince from a distance[5]. He was sitting on top of the wall, legs dangling[6]. And I heard him talking. "Don't you remember?" he was saying. "This isn't exactly the place!" Another voice must have answered him then, for he replied, "Oh yes, it's the right day, but this isn't the place . . ."

I continued walking toward the wall. I still could neither see nor hear anyone, yet the little prince answered again: "Of course. You'll see where my tracks[7] begin on the sand. Just wait for me there. I'll be there tonight."

I was twenty yards[8] from the wall and still saw no one.

Then the little prince said, after a silence, "Your poison[9] is good? You're sure it won't make me suffer[10] long?"

I stopped short, my heart pounding[11], but I still didn't understand.

70

"Now go away," the little prince said. "I want to get down from here!"

Then I looked down toward the foot of the wall, and gave a great start[1]! There, coiled in front of the little prince, was one of those yellow snakes that can kill you in thirty seconds.

As I dug into my pocket for my revolver[2], I stepped back, but at the noise I made, the snake flowed over the sand like a trickling[3] fountain[4], and without even hurrying, slipped away[5] between the stones with a faint[6] metallic[7] sound.

I reached the wall just in time to catch my little prince in my arms, his face white as snow.

"What's going on here? You're talking to snakes now?"

---

1. **give a start** 嚇了一跳
2. **revolver** [rɪ`vɑ:lvər] (n.) 左輪手槍
3. **trickle** [`trɪkəl] (v.) 細細地流
4. **fountain** [`faʊntn] (n.) 噴泉；泉水
5. **slip away** 滑走
6. **faint** [feɪnt] (a.) 微弱的
7. **metallic** [mə`tælɪk] (a.) 金屬的

"Now go away . . . I want to get down from here!"

71

I had loosened[1] the yellow scarf he always wore. I had moistened[2] his temples[3] and made him drink some water. And now I didn't dare ask him anything more. He gazed at me with a serious expression and put his arms round my neck. I felt his heart beating like a dying bird's, when it's been shot. He said to me:

"I'm glad you found what was the matter with your engine. Now you'll be able to fly again . . ."

"How did you know?" I was just coming to tell him that I had been successful beyond all hope!

He didn't answer my question; all he said was,"I'm leaving today, too." And then, sadly, "It's much further . . . It's much more difficult."

I realized that something extraordinary was happening. I was holding him in my arms like a little child, yet it seemed to me that he was dropping[4] headlong[5] into an abyss[6], and I could do nothing to hold him back.

---

1. **loosen** [`lu:sən] (v.) 鬆開
2. **moisten** [`mɔɪsən] (v.) 弄濕；使濕潤
3. **temple** [`tempəl] (n.) 太陽穴
4. **drop** [drɑ:p] (v.) 滴下
5. **headlong** [`hedlɑ:ŋ] (adv.) 頭朝前地；猛然地
6. **abyss** [ə`bɪs] (n.) 深淵；深坑

His expression was very serious now, lost and remote[7]. "I have your sheep. And I have the crate for it. And the muzzle . . ." And he smiled sadly.

I waited a long time. I could feel that he was reviving[8] a little. "Little fellow, you were frightened . . ." Of course he was frightened!

But he laughed a little. "I'll be much more frightened tonight . . ."

Once again I felt chilled[9] by the sense of something irreparable[10]. And I realized I couldn't bear[11] the thought of never hearing that laugh again. For me it was like a spring[12] of fresh water in the desert.

---

7. **remote** [rɪˋmout] (a.) 冷淡的
8. **revive** [rɪˋvaɪv] (v.) 恢復精力
9. **chilled** [tʃɪld] (a.) 冷的
10. **irreparable** [ɪˋrepərəbəl] (a.) 不能挽回的
11. **bear** [ber] (v.) 承受
12. **spring** [sprɪŋ] (n.) 泉

72

"Little fellow, I want to hear you laugh again . . ."

But he said to me, "Tonight, it'll be a year. My star will be just above the place where I fell last year . . ."

"Little fellow, it's a bad dream, isn't it? All this conversation[1] with the snake and the meeting place and the star . . ."

But he didn't answer my question. All he said was, "The important thing is what can't be seen . . ."

"Of course . . ."

"It's the same as for the flower. If you love a flower that lives on a star, then it's good, at night, to look up at the sky. All the stars are blossoming[2]."

"Of course . . ."

"It's the same for the water. The water you gave me to drink was like music, on account of the pulley and the rope. . . You remember . . . It was good."

"Of course . . ."

"At night, you'll look up at the stars. It's too small, where I live, for me to show you where my star is. It's better that way. My star will be. . . one of the stars, for you. So you'll like looking at all of them. They'll all be your friends. And besides[3], I have a present for you." He laughed again.

"Ah, little fellow, little fellow, I love hearing that laugh!"

"That'll be my present. Just that . . . It'll be the same as for the water."

"What do you mean?"

"People have stars, but they aren't the same. For travelers, the stars are guides[4]. For other people, they're nothing but tiny lights. And for still others, for scholars, they're problems[5]. For my businessman, they were gold. But all those stars are silent stars. You, though[6], you'll have stars like nobody else."

---

1. **conversation** [ˌkɑnvərˋseɪʃən] (n.) 談話；對話
2. **blossom** [ˋblɑ:səm] (v.) 出現；繁盛
3. **besides** [bɪˋsaɪdz] (adv.) 除此之外
4. **guide** [gaɪd] (n.) 嚮導
5. **problem** [ˋprɑ:bləm] (n.) 難題；疑問
6. **though** [ðoʊ] (adv.) 然而

73

"What do you mean?"

"When you look up at the sky at night, since I'll be living on one of them, since I'll be laughing on one of them, for you it'll be as if all the stars are laughing. You'll have stars that can laugh!"

And he laughed again.

"And when you're consoled[1] (everyone eventually[2] is consoled), you'll be glad you've known me. You'll always be my friend. You'll feel like laughing with me. And you'll open your window sometimes just for the fun of it. . . And your friends will be amazed to see you laughing while you're looking up at the sky. Then you'll tell them, 'Yes, it's the stars; they always make me laugh!' And they'll think you're crazy. It'll be a nasty[3] trick[4] I played on you . . ."

And he laughed again.

"And it'll be as if I had given you, instead of stars, a lot of tiny[5] bells that know how to laugh . . ."

And he laughed again. Then he grew serious once more. "Tonight . . . you know . . . don't come."

"I won't leave you."

"It'll look as if[6] I'm suffering. It'll look a little as if I'm dying. It'll look that way. Don't come to see that; it's not worth the trouble."

"I won't leave you."

But he was anxious[7]. "I'm telling you this . . . on account of the snake. He mustn't bite[8] you. Snakes are nasty sometimes. They bite just for fun . . ."

"I won't leave you."

But something reassured him. "It's true they don't have enough poison for a second bite . . ."

---

1. **console** [kən`soul] (v.) 安慰；撫慰
2. **eventually** [ɪ`ventʃuəli] (adv.) 最後；最終
3. **nasty** [`næsti] (a.) 令人討厭的；令人難受的
4. **trick** [trɪk] (n.) 詭計；惡作劇
5. **tiny** [`taɪni] (a.) 極小的；微小的
6. **look as if** 使看起來似乎……
7. **anxious** [`æŋkʃəs] (a.) 焦慮的
8. **bite** [baɪt] (v.) 咬 (bite-bit-bit)

74

That night I didn't see him leave. He got away[1] without making a sound. When I managed to[2] catch up with[3] him, he was walking fast, with determination[4]. All he said was, "Ah, you're here." And he took my hand. But he was still anxious. "You were wrong to come. You'll suffer. I'll look as if I'm dead, and that won't be true . . ."

I said nothing.

"You understand. It's too far. I can't take this body with me. It's too heavy."

I said nothing.

"But it'll be like an old abandoned[5] shell. There's nothing sad about an old shell . . ."

I said nothing.

He was a little disheartened[6] now. But he made one more effort.

---

1. **get away** 離開
2. **manage + to** 設法做到；勉強完成
3. **catch up with** 趕上
4. **determination** [dɪˏtɜ:rmɪˋneɪʃən] (n.) 堅定；果決
5. **abandoned** [əˋbændənd] (a.) 被遺棄的
6. **dishearten** [dɪsˋhɑ:rtn] (v.) 使氣餒；使沮喪
7. **rusty** [ˋrʌsti] (a.) 生鏽的
8. **pour** [pɔ:r] (v.) 倒；灌

"It'll be nice, you know. I'll be looking at the stars, too. All the stars will be wells with a rusty[7] pulley. All the stars will pour[8] out water for me to drink . . ."

I said nothing.

"And it'll be fun! You'll have five-hundred million little bells; I'll have five-hundred million springs of fresh water . . ." And he, too, said nothing, because he was weeping . . . .

And he sat down because he was frightened.

"Here's the place. Let me go on alone."

And he sat down because he was frightened.

Then he said: "You know . . . my flower . . . I'm responsible for her. And she's so weak! And so naive[1]. She has four ridiculous thorns to defend her against the world . . ."

I sat down, too, because I was unable to stand any longer.

He said, "There . . . That's all . . ."

He hesitated[2] a little longer, then he stood up. He took a step. I couldn't move.

There was nothing but a yellow flash[3] close to his ankle. He remained motionless[4] for an instant[5]. He didn't cry out. He fell gently[6], the way a tree falls. There wasn't even a sound, because of the sand.

---

1. **naive** [naɪˋi:v] (a.) 天真的；幼稚的
2. **hesitate** [ˋhezəteɪt] (v.) 躊躇；猶豫
3. **flash** [flæʃ] (n.) 閃光
4. **motionless** [ˋmoʊʃənləs] (a.) 不動的；靜止的
5. **for an instant** 頃刻；一瞬間
6. **gently** [ˋdʒentli] (adv.) 輕輕地；和緩地

76

27

And now, of course, it's been six years already . . . I've never told this story before. The friends who saw me again were very glad to see me alive. I was sad, but I told them, "It's fatigue[1]."

Now I'm somewhat[2] consoled. That is . . . not entirely[3]. But I know he did get back to his planet because at daybreak I didn't find his body. It wasn't such a heavy body . . . And at night I love listening to the stars. It's like five-hundred million little bells . . . .

---

1. **fatigue** [fə`ti:g] (n.) 勞累；疲憊
2. **somewhat** [`sʌmwa:t] (adv.) 有點；稍微
3. **entirely** [ɪn`taɪrli] (adv.) 完全地；徹底地
4. **leather strap** 皮帶
5. **fasten** [`fæsən] (v.) 繫緊
6. **distract** [dɪ`strækt] (v.) 使分心

But something extraordinary has happened. When I drew that muzzle for the little prince, I forgot to put in the leather strap[4]. He could never have fastened[5] it on his sheep.

And then I wonder, "What's happened there on his planet? Maybe the sheep has eaten the flower . . ."

Sometimes I tell myself, "Of course not! The little prince puts his flower under glass, and he keeps close watch over his sheep. . ." Then I'm happy. And all the stars laugh sweetly.

Sometimes I tell myself, "Anyone might be distracted[6] once in a while, and that's all it takes! One night he forgot to put her under glass, or else the sheep got out without making any noise, during the night . . ." Then the bells are all changed into tears!

He fell gently, the way a tree falls.
There wasn't even a sound...

It's all a great mystery. For you, who love the little prince, too. As for me, nothing in the universe can be the same if somewhere, no one knows where, a sheep we never saw has or has not eaten a rose . . .

Look up at the sky. Ask yourself, "Has the sheep eaten the flower or not?"

And you'll see how everything changes . . .

And no grown-up will ever understand how such a thing could be so important!

For me, this is the loveliest[1] and the saddest landscape in the world. It's the same landscape as the one on the preceding[2] page, but I've drawn it one more time in order to be sure you see it clearly. It's here that the little prince appeared on Earth, then disappeared.

Look at this landscape carefully to be sure of recognizing[3] it, if you should travel to Africa someday, in the desert. And if you happen to[4] pass by here, I beg you not to hurry past. Wait a little, just under the star! Then if a child comes to you, if he laughs, if he has golden hair, if he doesn't answer your questions, you'll know who he is. If this should happen, be kind! Don't let me go on being so sad: Send word[5] immediately[6] that he's come back . . . .

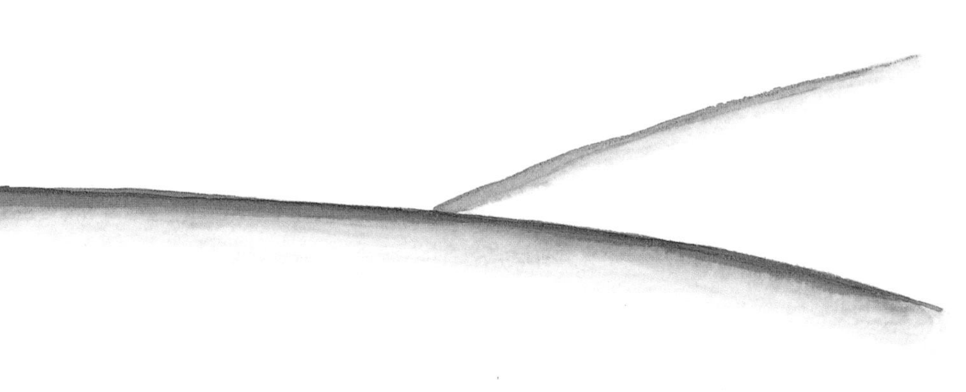

1. **loveliest** [`lʌvlɪst]
(a.)（lovely 的最高級）最可愛的
2. **preceding** [pri`si:dɪŋ]
(a.) 在前面的
3. **recognize** [`rekəgnaɪz]
(v.) 確認；認出
4. **happen + to** 偶然發生
5. **word** [wɜ:rd] (n.)
文字；信息
6. **immediately** [ɪ`mi:diətli]
(adv.) 即刻地；直接地

Beautiful Quotes
From *The Little Prince*

If someone loves a flower of which just one example exists among all the millions and millions of stars, that's enough to make him happy when he looks at the stars.

假如一個人愛上了一朵花，那是數千數百萬顆星星裡的一朵花，當他看著這些星星時就足以讓他快樂不已了。

I should have judged her according to her actions, not her words. She perfumed my planet and lit up my life.

我應該根據她的行為去了解她，而不是她的言語。她使我的星球充滿芬芳，也照亮了我的生命。

"Where are the people? It's a little lonely in the desert . . ."

"It's also lonely with people." said the snake.

「人兒在哪裡？在沙漠裡有點寂寞……」

「在人群之中也很寂寞。」蛇這樣說道。

But if you tame me, we'll need each other. You'll be the only boy in the world for me. I'll be the only fox in the world for you . . .

但是假如你豢養我，我們就會互相需要。你對我來說，是世界上獨一無二的男孩。而我對你來說，也是世界上獨一無二的狐狸……

It would have been better to return at the same time. For instance, if you come at four in the afternoon, I'll begin to be happy by three. The closer it gets to four, the happier I'll feel.

你最好每天按時回來。例如，假如你下午四點回來，我三點就會開始高興了起來。愈接近四點的時候，我就會愈雀躍。

One sees clearly only with the heart. Anything essential is invisible to the eyes.

人只有用心靈才看得清楚，重要的東西是肉眼看不見的。

What makes the desert beautiful is that it hides a well somewhere . . .

讓這片沙漠美麗的原因是因為某處藏了一座井……

People where you live grow five thousand roses in one garden . . . yet they don't find what they're looking for . . . And yet what they're looking for could be found in a single rose, or a little water . . .

你那裡的人在一個花園種了五百朵玫瑰……然而，他們都不知道自己在尋找什麼……他們尋找的可能就在一朵玫瑰花裡，或幾滴的水之中……

When you look up at the sky at night, since I'll be living on one of them, since I'll be laughing on one of them, for you it'll be as if all the stars are laughing.

當你在夜晚抬頭看著天空時，因為我住在其中一顆星球的緣故，因為我會在星球裡微笑著，你就會覺得所有的星球都在對你微笑。

Appendixes

1. Basic Grammar
2. Guide to Listening Comprehension
3. Listening Guide
4. Listening Comprehension

Appendix 1

Basic Grammar

要增強英文閱讀理解能力，應練習找出英文的主結構。
要擁有良好的英語閱讀能力，首先要理解英文的段落結構。

英文的閱讀理解從「分解文章」開始

英文的文章是以「有意義的詞組」（指帶有意義的語句）所構成的。用（／）符號來區別各個意義語塊，請試著掌握其中的意義。

He knew / that she told a lie / at the party.

他知道　她說了謊　在舞會上

⇨ 他知道她在舞會上說謊的事。

As she was walking / in the garden, / she smelled / something wet.

當她行走　在花園　她聞到味道　某樣東西濕濕的

⇨ 她走在花園時聞到潮溼的味道。

一篇文章，要分成幾個有意義的詞組？

可放入（／）符號來區隔有意義詞組的地方，一般是在（1）「主詞＋動詞」之後；（2）and 和 but 等連接詞之前；（3）that、who 等關係代名詞之前；（4）副詞子句的前後，會用（／）符號來區隔。初學者可能在一篇文章中畫很多（／）符號，但隨著閱讀實力的提升，（／）會減少。時間一久，在不太複雜的文章中即使不畫（／）符號，也能一眼就理解整句的意義。

使用（／）符號來閱讀理解英語篇章

1. 能熟悉英文的句型和構造；
2. 可加速閱讀速度。

該方法對於需要邊聽理解的英文聽力也有很好的效果。
從現在開始，早日丟棄過去理解文章的習慣吧！

以直接閱讀理解的方式，重新閱讀《小王子》

從原文中摘錄一小段。以具有意義的詞組將文章做斷句區分，重新閱讀並做理解練習。

Once when I was six / I saw a magnificent picture / in a book about the jungle, / called True Stories. //
我六歲的時候　我看到一幅壯觀的圖畫　在關於叢林的一本書裡　叫做《真實的故事》

It showed a boa constrictor / swallowing a wild beast. //
上面是一隻大蟒蛇　吞掉一隻野獸

Here is / a copy of the picture. //
這裡是　圖畫的複製品

In the book / it said: / "Boa constrictors swallow their prey whole, / without chewing. //
在這本書裡　它提到　「大蟒蛇吞掉牠們整隻的獵食　連嚼都沒嚼

Afterward / they are no longer able to move, / and they sleep for six months / they need for digestion." //
之後　牠們再也不能移動　牠們沉睡了六個月
牠們需要時間來消化

In those days / I thought a lot about jungle adventures, / and eventually managed to make my first drawing / with a colored pencil. //
在那些日子　我想了很多關於叢林冒險的事
最後決定畫我的第一張圖畫　用一枝彩色鉛筆

My drawing Number One / looked like this: //
我的《第一號繪畫作品》　看起來像這樣：

I showed the grown-ups my masterpiece, / and I asked them / if my drawing scared them. //
我把我的傑作給大人看　然後我問他們
我的畫是否嚇到了他們

They answered, / "Why should anyone be scared / of a hat?" //
他們回答，　「為什麼有人會害怕　一頂帽子？」

My drawing was not a picture of a hat. //
我的繪畫不是在畫帽子

It was a picture of a boa constrictor / digesting an elephant. //
它是畫一條大蟒蛇　吞掉了一頭大象

Then / I drew the inside of the boa constrictor, / so the grown-ups could understand. //
然後　我畫了大蟒蛇的內部　這樣大人就懂了

They always need explanations. //
他們總是需要別人的說明

The grown-ups advised me / to put away my drawings / of boa constrictors, outside or inside, / and apply myself instead / to geography, history, arithmetic, and grammar. //

大人建議我　把我的圖畫收好　大蟒蛇外部的或內部的　轉而專心　於地理、歷史、算術，和文法

That is why I gave up, / at the age of six, / a magnificent career as an artist. //
這就是為什麼我放棄　在六歲時　當一個畫家這個偉大志向的職業

I had been discouraged / by the failure of my drawing Number One and of my drawing Number Two. //
我被挫敗　因為我的《第一號繪畫作品》和《第二號繪畫作品》的失敗

Grown-ups never understand anything / by themselves, / and it is exhausting / for children to have to explain / over and over again. //
大人從不了解任何事　靠他們自己　很累人　因為小孩總要解釋　再三地

So then / I had to choose another career. //
所以之後　我必須選擇另一個職業

I learned to pilot airplanes. //
我學習駕駛飛機

I have flown / almost everywhere in the world. //
我駕駛飛機　幾乎到世界各地

As a matter of fact, / geography has been a big help / to me. //
事實上　地理學有很大的幫助　對我而言

I could tell China from Arizona / at first glance, / which is very useful / if you get lost / during the night. //
我能分辨中國和美國的亞利桑那州　看一眼　是很有用的　假如你迷航　在夜晚時分

So I have met, / in the course of my life, / lots of serious people. //
所以我遇見了　我人生中　很多重要的人

Appendix 2

Guide to Listening Comprehension

When listening to the story, use some of the techniques shown below. If you take time to study some phonetic characteristics of English, listening will be easier.

Get in the flow of English.

English creates a rhythm formed by combinations of strong and weak stress intonations. Each word has its particular stress that combines with other words to form the overall pattern of stress or rhythm in a particular sentence.

When speaking and listening to English, it is essential to get in the flow of the rhythm of English. It takes a lot of practice to get used to such a rhythm. So, you need to start by identifying the stressed syllable in a word.

Listen for the strongly stressed words and phrases.

In English, key words and phrases that are essential to the meaning of a sentence are stressed louder. Therefore, pay attention to the words stressed with a higher pitch. When listening to an English recording for the first time, what matters most is to listen for a general understanding of what you hear. Do not try to hear every single word. Most of the unstressed words are articles or auxiliary verbs, which don't play an important role in the general context. At this level, you can ignore them.

Pay attention to liaisons.

In reading English, words are written with a space between them. There isn't such an obvious guide when it comes to listening to English. In oral English, there are many cases when the sounds of words are linked with adjacent words.

For instance, let's think about the phrase "**take off**," which can be used in "take off your clothes." "Take off your clothes" doesn't sound like [teək ɔ:f] with each of the words completely and clearly separated from the others. Instead, it sounds as if almost all the words in context are slurred together, [`teəkɔ:f], for a more natural sound.

Shadow the voice of the native speaker.

Finally, you need to mimic the voice of the native speaker. Once you are sure you know how to pronounce all the words in a sentence, try to repeat them like an echo. Listen to the book again, but this time you should try a fun exercise while listening to the English.

This exercise is called "shadowing." The word "shadow" means a dark shade that is formed on a surface. When used as a verb, the word refers to the action of following someone or something like a shadow. In this exercise, pretend you are a parrot and try to shadow the voice of the native speaker.

Try to mimic the reader's voice by speaking at the same speed, with the same strong and weak stresses on words, and pausing or stopping at the same points.

Experts have already proven this technique to be effective. If you practice this shadowing exercise, your English speaking and listening skills will improve by leaps and bounds. While shadowing the native speaker, don't forget to pay attention to the meaning of each phrase and sentence.

Listen to what you want to shadow many times. Start out by just trying to shadow a few words or a sentence.

Mimic the CD out loud. You can shadow everything the speaker says as if you are singing a round, or you also can speak simultaneously with the recorded voice of the native speaker.

As you practice more, try to shadow more. For instance, shadow a whole sentence or paragraph instead of just a few words.

Appendix

3 Listening Guide

以下為《小王子》各章節的前半部。一開始若能聽清楚發音，之後就沒有聽力的負擔。首先，請聽過摘錄的章節，之後再反覆聆聽括弧內單字的發音，並仔細閱讀各種發音的說明。

以下都是以英語的典型發音為基礎，所做的簡易說明，即使這裡未提到的發音，也可以配合 CD 反覆聆聽，如此一來聽力必能更上層樓。

Chapter One page 12 (79)

Once (❶) ( ) ( ) ( ) I saw a magnificent picture in a book about the jungle, called *True Stories*. It showed a boa constrictor swallowing a (❷) ( ). Here is a copy of the picture. In the book it said: "Boa constrictors swallow their prey whole, without chewing. Afterward they are no longer able to move, and they sleep for six months they need for digestion."

In those days I thought (❸) ( ) ( ) jungle adventures, and (❹) ( ) ( ) make my first drawing with a colored pencil. My drawing *Number One* looked like this:
I showed the grown-ups my masterpiece, and I asked them if my drawing (❺) ( ). They answered, "Why should anyone be scared of a hat?"

My drawing was not a picture of a hat. It was a picture of a boa constrictor digesting an elephant.

❶ **When I was six:** was 和 six 連在一起發音時，s 因前後重複，故只發音一次，was 的發音較弱。此句的重音落在 six，所以其他的音聽起來會相對微弱。

❷ **wild beast:** wild 和 beast 連在一起發音時，wild 的 [d] 音會呈現其發音的嘴型，但略過不發，beast 中的 -st 為無聲子音，發音聽起來微弱。

❸ **a lot about:** lot 與 about 合在一起發音時，lot 的 [t] 音與 about 的 [ə] 音會產生連音，唸起來就不完全是 ta 的音，而是一種介於 ta 和 da 之間的音。此連音現象為英語發音中的常見現象，應予熟記。而此句中，about 的 [t] 音也會略過不發。

❹ **eventually managed to:** eventually 的重音在第二音節，第一音節的母音聽不清楚，聽起來會像是 ventually 的發音。

managed 與 to 連在一起發音時，managed 的 -d 音會略過不發，所以須根據上下文來判斷時態。

❺ **scared them:** scared 與 them 連在一起發音時，scared 的 [d] 音與 them 的 [ð] 音會產生連音。

Chapter One page 13–15 80

Then I drew the inside of the boa constrictor, so the grown-ups (❶) ( ). They always need explanations.

My drawing *Number Two* (❷) ( ) ( ):
The grown-ups advised me to (❸) ( ) my drawings of boa constrictors, outside or inside, and apply myself instead to geography, history, arithmetic, and grammar. That is why I (❹) ( ), at the age of six, a magnificent (❺) ( ) ( ) ( ). I had been discouraged by the failure of my drawing *Number One* and of my drawing *Number Two*.

Grown-ups never understand anything by themselves, and it is exhausting for children to have to explain over and over again.

So then I had to choose another career. I (❻) ( ) pilot airplanes. I have flown almost everywhere in the world. And, (❼) ( ) ( ) ( ) ( ), geography has been a (❽) ( ) to me. I could tell China from Arizona at (❾) ( ), which is very useful if you get lost during the night.

❶ **could understand:** could 以及發音類似的助 詞 should、would 等，子尾的 [d] 音通常發音很輕或只出現嘴型而略過不發，需依據前後文來判斷其發音。同樣地，understand 的 [d] 音通常略過而聽不出其發音。

❷ **looked like this:** looked 的 -ed 發 [t] 音，looked 發 [lukt] 音，與後面 like 連在一起發音時， [k] 會略過不發出聲音。

❸ **put away:** put 和 away 連在一起發音，put 的 [t] 音和 away 的 [ə] 音會產生連音，唸起來是一種介於 ta 和 da 之間的音。

❹ **gave up:** gave up 是 give up 的過去式，give 與 up 連在一起發音時，gave 的 v 音與 up 會產生連音。同樣地，give up 的 v 音也是如此。而 up 的 [p] 音則略過不發。

❺ **career as an artist:** career 的尾音 [r] 和後面的 as 連在一起發，會迅速略過。as 的 [s] 音和 an 會產生連音 [sən] 。而 artist 的 -st 的音非常微弱，必須專注聽才聽得出來。career as a/an 為常用句型，as 與 a/an 均會產生連音。

❻ **learned to:** learned 與 to 連在一起發音時，learned 的 -ed 音通常迅速略過，必須根據上下文來判斷時態。

❼ **as a matter of fact:** as 的 -s 與 a 會產生連音，matter 的 -r 與 of 的 o 產生連音。而 of 和 fact 重複的 [f] 音，只發出一個 [f] 音。fact 的 [t] 音在日常生活對話中常迅速略過而聽不出來。

❽ **big help:** big 的 [g] 音通常做出嘴型，但不發出聲音。help 的 [p] 音常迅速略過而聽不出其發音。

❾ **first glance:** first 與 glance 連在一起發音時，first 的 -t 音會略過不發。

Appendix

4 Listening Comprehension

81 A Listen to the CD and fill in the blanks.

1. The little prince did not know much about Earth. He was ______________. .
2. A snake had ______________ for the little prince in the desert.
3. The author of this story landed in the desert because his plane had ______________ problems.
4. The little prince thought that the lamplighter is a fine ______________.
5. The author could draw boa constrictors from the ______________ and inside.
6. The little prince liked to watch ______________ on his planet.

82 B True or False.

T F 1 ....

T F 2 ....

T F 3 ....

T F 4 ....

T F 5 ....

T F 6 ....

83 **C** Listen to the CD and choose the correct answer.

❶ ____?

(a) He was bored.

(b) He thought he owned them.

(c) He wanted to sell all of them.

❷ ____?

(a) He forgot to color it brown.

(b) He forgot to give the drawing to the little prince.

(c) He forgot to draw a strap for the muzzle.

84 **D** Listen to the CD and write down the sentences. Rearrange the sentences in chronological order.

1 ....

2 ....

3 ....

4 ....

5 ....

________ ⇨ ________ ⇨ ________ ⇨ ________ ⇨ ________

Translation

作者簡介

p. 8 安托萬・德・聖艾修伯里出生在貴族家庭，度過快樂的童年。1921 年，他加入法國空軍，成為飛行員。結束軍人生活後，他一邊找尋工作，一邊為雜誌書寫。為了逃脫日常生活，1926 年，聖艾修伯里開始駕駛飛機，為史上最初的空運郵務員。這些飛行經歷提供他創作《南方郵航》（*Southern Mail*）和《夜間飛行》（*Night Flight*）的養分。《夜間飛行》獲頒費米娜文學獎，並受當代作家的讚譽。

聖艾修伯里的著作藉著克服一切困難挑戰的飛行，反映尋找人生意義的過程。二戰爆發，他負責以空軍監控，德國佔領法國後，他被放逐至美國，在那撰寫了《小王子》（*The Little Prince*）。

1942 年時，聖艾修伯里為了同盟國的勝利，再次加入空軍。1944 年 7 月 31 日，為了收集德國軍隊在羅納河谷行動的資料，他在夜間起飛，便從此消失。《小王子》與他其餘飽受喜愛的著作，都被翻譯成多國語言並成為經典。

故事介紹

p. 9 1943 年，被放逐美國的安托萬・德・聖艾修伯里寫下《小王子》，提供讀者奇幻與詩意的色彩，是給大人看的童話故事。聖艾修伯里寫作汲取身為飛行員的經歷，包括他在撒哈拉沙漠墜落的故事。

故事的敘述者，同作者是個飛行員，被困在廣大無際的沙漠裡，並遇到了從一顆小行星前來的小王子。因為一朵美麗又彆扭的玫瑰，小王子感到沮喪並開始旅程。經過漫長的旅途，他到達地球，遇上一隻狐狸。狐狸教導他，只有心靈才能看見真正重要的事物。小王子瞭解到，人生中真正重要的事物，有時肉眼是看不到的，而他也才明白了玫瑰的真實價值。

聖艾修伯里利用小王子旅途中的角色，傳達出人長大後，那些無法看見或容易忘記的珍貴的人生價值。《小王子》也反映出作者所主張，生命意義即在人際連結中的概念。作者美麗的插圖也為故事帶來詩意的氛圍與人性的溫度。

p. 11 獻給利昂・瑞斯

我希望喜愛這本書的小孩能諒解我將此書獻給一位大人，我有一個很重要的理由：他是我在這世界上最好的朋友。另一個理由是：這個大人無所不知，甚至包括童書。第三個理由是：他住在法國，他在那裡既餓又冷，很需要鼓勵。假如以上的理由還不夠充分的話，那我就將這本書獻給這個大人還未長大時的那個小孩。所有的大人都曾經是小孩——雖然很少人記得這個事實。所以我修正我的獻詞：

獻給利昂・瑞斯
當他還是小男孩的時候

1

p. 12–13 我六歲那年，看過一本故事書，書名叫《真實的故事》，內容是描述有關原始森林的生態，裡面有一幅非常壯觀的圖畫。那是一條大蟒蛇正在吞食獵物的畫面，這張圖是我模仿它而畫的。

書上說：「大蟒蛇嚼也不嚼地就將整隻獵物吞下。吞下後，牠們便再也無法動彈，必須用上整整六個月的時間，一面睡覺一面消化獵物。」

那時我一直在想著這段叢林奇遇，最後就拿起一枝彩色鉛筆，第一次地把它畫了出來，我把它編為《第一號繪畫作品》，就像這個樣子：

我把這個傑作拿給大人們看，並問他們害不害怕。沒想到他們卻回答：「害怕？一頂帽子有什麼好怕的呢？」

我畫的並不是一頂帽子，而是一條正在消化一隻大象的大蟒蛇。於是我又畫了一張：我把大蟒蛇內部的樣子畫出來，好讓大人可以看清楚。大人們習慣每件事情都需要說明。

p. 14–15 這是我的《第二號繪畫作品》：

大人們告訴我說，不管是不是可以看得到裡面，以後不要再畫大蟒蛇了，應該專心研讀地理、歷史、算術和文法才對。也因此，在六歲時，我就放棄了成為一位偉大畫家的打算。第一號和第二號作品的失敗，讓我感到很洩氣。

大人們什麼都不懂，小孩子要這樣再三地向他們解釋，實在是很累。

於是我選擇了另一種職業——開飛機。世界上的每個角落我幾乎都飛遍了，地理學的知識也確實派上了用場。只要瞄一眼，我就可以分辨出是飛在中國還是亞利桑那州的上空，這一招在夜間迷航時特別有效。

這輩子，我遇見過很多正經八百的人，也和大人們相處過不少時間，和他們很近距離地接觸過，只是那並沒有改變多少我對他們的看法。

p. 16 有時，遇到看起來比較有見識的，我會拿出我一直保存著的《第一號繪畫作品》，看他是否真能看懂什麼。

但我得到的答案總是：「這是一頂帽子。」這樣我就不會跟那個人提起大蟒蛇、原始叢林或星星。我會配合他的水準，只聊些橋牌、高爾夫球、政治和領帶之類的話題，而他則會非常高興，能遇到一位如此通情達理的人。

2

p. 17 因此，我一直都是一個人過活，沒有什麼真正談得來的朋友。直到六年前，有一次我的飛機引擎發生故障，在撒哈拉沙漠中迫降。當時，因為既沒有機械師，也沒有任何旅客與我同行，我只好獨力進行艱鉅的修復工作。對我來說，這是攸關生死的大事：我所帶的飲水僅足夠維持八天左右。

第一天晚上，我就睡在遠離人煙千里之遙的沙地上，這比在海難中坐著救生艇、漂流在大海上，還更讓人感覺到孤絕。所以，你不難想像，黎明時分，當我被一陣微弱的怪聲音給吵醒時，我會有多麼地詫異了。那個聲音說道：「可否請你……幫我畫一隻綿羊……」

p. 18–19 「什麼？」

「畫一隻綿羊……」我像被雷打到一樣地倏然跳起。我用力地揉揉眼睛，張大眼睛看，我看到一個個頭非常小的小傢伙，正一臉正經地盯著我看。這一幅畫是事後我為他畫的肖像畫中最好的一幅。

不過，圖畫看起來當然沒有他本人來得吸引人。但這也不能怪我，自從我六歲那年，大人們打消了我想當畫家的念頭後，除了大蟒蛇的外觀和內部之外，我就沒再畫過任何東西了。

於是我睜大眼睛看著這個幻影。別忘了，我當時正身處在人煙千里之外的沙漠中。然而，這個小傢伙看起來不像是在沙漠中迷路的樣子，他看起來不累不飢不渴，也沒有一副會害怕死在沙漠之中的樣子。他實在一點也不像是在沙漠中走失的小孩——在離塵囂千里之遙的沙漠中。

p. 20–21 當我終於能開口講話的時候，我說：「可是……你在這裡做什麼？」

他很正經地慢慢重複道：「可否請你……幫我畫一隻綿羊……」

人在遇到很奇怪的事情時，是不會去違抗指示的。雖然這想起來實在是很荒謬——在遠離人煙千里之外並有死亡之虞的當頭，我從口袋裡拿出了一張紙和一枝筆，但就在此時，我想起自己只學過地理、歷史、算術和文法，所以我跟小傢伙說（帶著不悅的語氣），我不會畫畫。

他回答我說：「那沒關係！幫我畫一隻綿羊。」

因為我沒畫過綿羊，所以我就畫了我只會畫的那兩張圖當中的一張——大蟒蛇的外觀。當我聽見小傢伙看到畫的反應時，我嚇了一跳。

「不！不！我要的不是一隻在大蟒蛇肚子裡的大象。大蟒蛇太危險，大象太笨重，我住的地方，每樣東西都很小，我要的是一隻綿羊，幫我畫一隻綿羊。」

既然如此，我就畫了一隻綿羊。

他仔細地看了看，然後說：「不！這隻羊看起來病懨懨的，幫我再畫一張。」

p. 22–23 於是，我又畫了一張。我這位朋友好心溫和地笑了笑。

「你自己看……」他說：「這不是綿羊，這是一隻公羊，牠的頭上有長角。」

因此，我又重新畫了一張，但還是未能合他的意。

「這隻太老了，我想要一隻可以活很久的綿羊。」

這時，我的耐心快被磨光了，因為我得趕緊去修理飛機引擎。我草草地畫了這張圖，並解釋道：「這是裝著牠的箱子，你要的綿羊就在裡面。」

沒想到，我的小鑑賞家竟面露喜色地說：「這正是我想要的！你想牠需要吃很多的草嗎？」

「為什麼這麼問？」

「因為我住的地方，每樣東西都很小……」

「草是夠牠吃的。」我說：「我畫給你的是一隻非常小的綿羊。」

他低頭端詳著圖畫：「沒那麼小……你看！牠睡著了……」

這就是我認識小王子的經過。

3

p. 24–25 我花了不少時間才搞清楚他是從哪來的。小王子問了我很多問題，而我問他的問題他好像都沒聽進去。

關於小王子，我是從他的談話當中一點一滴慢慢拼湊出來的。例如，他第一次看到我的飛機時（飛機對我來說太複雜，我就不畫了），他問我：

「那是什麼東西呀？」

「那不是東西，它可以飛，是一架飛機，我的飛機。」

我很得意讓他知道我會飛行。他立即叫道：「什麼？你是從天上掉下來的？」

「沒錯！」我謙虛地答道。

「噢！好奇怪喔……」小王子開心地哈哈大笑，這讓我很生氣。我希望別人知道我的不幸時，在態度上能夠正經一點。過了一會，他又說：「這麼說來，你也是從天上來的！你是從哪一個星球來的？」

p. 26-27 這時，對於他的神秘來歷，我有了一點頭緒。我直截地問道：「你是從別的星球來的嗎？」

他沒有回答，只是盯著我的飛機，微微地搖著頭說：「也對，坐在這個東西上面，是不可能從太遠的地方來的……」

之後他陷入遐思半晌，然後從口袋裡拿出我畫給他的綿羊，對著這個寶貝沈思了起來。

你不難想像，他那句煞有其事的「別的星球」的話，是如何地挑起了我的好奇心。我竭力想得到更多線索，「小傢伙，你是從哪裡來的？你所說的『我住的地方』是在哪裡？你要把綿羊帶到哪裡去？」

他靜靜地沈思了一會兒，說道：「你給我的這個箱子，綿羊在晚上時可以睡在裡面。」

「是啊！如果你聽話的話，我還會幫你畫一條繩子，白天時可以把牠拴起來，我還會再畫一根可以拴住牠的柱子。」

但我這個提議似乎讓他有些震驚。「拴住牠！這想法太奇怪了！」

我說：「如果不拴住牠，牠到處亂跑，就會走失的。」

我的朋友又噗嗤笑了出來。

「牠能會跑到哪裡去？」

「就到處跑，一直往前跑……」

小王子很正經地說道：「那也沒關係，我住的地方很小！」接著他有點無奈地又說：「一直往前跑，也不能跑多遠的……」

4

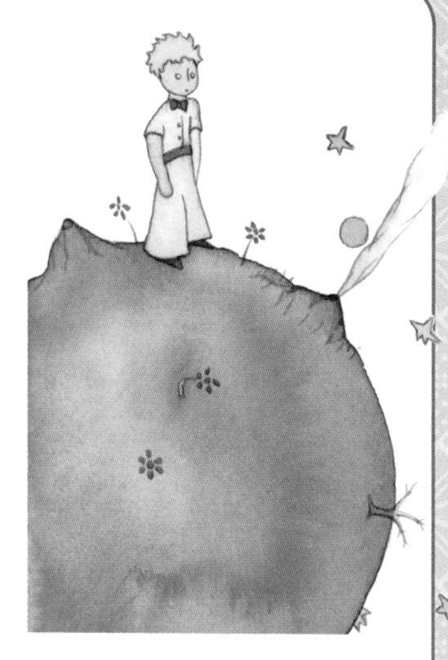

p. 28–28 於是，我得知了第二件重要的事：小王子所住的星球，比一棟房子大不了多少！

這我一點也不訝異。因為我很清楚，除了地球、木星、火星、金星這些有被命名的大行星之外，還有好幾百個很小的星球，用望遠鏡也很難發現到它們。而一旦它們被天文學家發現時，它們不會被命名，而是給它編個號碼，譬如「第 325 號小行星」。

我有很好的理由相信小王子來自「B-612 號小行星」。

這顆小行星 1909 年時曾被一位土耳其的天文學家用望遠鏡觀測過唯一的一次，這位天文學家曾在國際天文學會中舉證發表過，不過因為他身上穿的是土耳其服裝，所以沒有人肯相信他說的話。大人就是這樣。

p. 30–31 所幸，為了「B-612 號小行星」的名聲，一位土耳其的獨裁者就下令人民要改穿歐式的服裝，違者處死。1920 年，這位天文學家穿著高貴的歐式服裝，重新發表，結果這一次大家都接受他的說法了。

我會告訴你們這些 B-612 號小行星的細節和編號，那是因為大人們和他們做事習慣的緣故。大人們喜愛數字，當你告訴他們，你交了一位新朋友時，他們不會問你任何重要的問題。

譬如他們從來不問：「他的聲音聽起來怎樣？他最喜歡玩什麼遊戲？他蒐集蝴蝶嗎？」

相反地，他們會問：「他幾歲？有幾個兄弟？他體重多重？他父親的收入有多少？」

只有從這些數字當中，大人們才會認為對他有一些瞭解。假如你對大人們說：「我看到一棟用玫瑰色磚塊砌成的漂亮房子，窗台上擺著天竺葵，屋頂上停著白鴿。」他們對於這棟房子還是不會有任何概念，你必須跟他們說：「我看到一棟價值兩萬美金的房子。」這時，他們便會叫道：「真是一棟漂亮的房子啊！」

p. 32–33 同樣地，你如果對大人們說：「小王子存在的證明，就是他很可愛，他笑笑的，還有他想要一隻綿羊。某人想要一隻羊，就證明某人是存在過的。」大人們只會聳聳肩膀，把你當小孩子看待！

但如果你對他們說：「小王子來自 B-612 號小行星。」那麼，他們便會相信你的話，不會提出問題來糾纏你了。大人們就是這樣，不需要為此和他們唱反調，小孩子應該體諒大人的。

當然，像我們這種懂得生活的人，就不在乎數字了！我本想以童話的方式來寫這個故事，開頭就像這樣：「從前有一位小王子，他住在一個體積比他大不了多少的星球上，他想要一隻綿羊……」對那些懂得生活的來說，這聽起來真實得多了。

我不希望別人草草率率地讀我的書。回溯這些往事，是讓我很難過的。我的朋友帶著他的綿羊，離開我已經有六年了。

我在這裡盡力地描述他，好讓自己不要忘了他。把朋友給忘了，是一件很悲哀的事，並不是每個人都曾有過朋友的。我也許會變得跟大人一樣，除了數字外，不再對任何事情感到興趣。也就是為了這個緣故，我買了一盒顏料和幾枝鉛筆。到我這個年紀才重拾畫筆，不是一件簡單的事。尤其是自從六歲之後，除了那兩張大蟒蛇的內部和外觀的繪畫以外，我就再也不曾畫過任何東西了。

p. 34 我當然會盡力把肖像畫得栩栩如生，不過能不能成功，我就沒有把握了。有的畫得還不錯，有的則畫得一點也不像。就拿小王子的身高來說，我便拿捏不準：有時畫得太高，有時又太矮。還有衣服的顏色，我也不是很確定。

我只能儘量地揣摩，總之在某些重要的細節上，我一定有畫錯的地方，這要請大家見諒，因為我這個朋友，從來也不多加解說過什麼。或許他認為我跟他是同一類的，但很遺憾的，我是無法透過箱子看到裡面的綿羊的。我可能和大人們有點相像了，我一定是老了。

5

p. 36–37 每天我都會從我們的談話當中，獲知一些小王子星球上的事，以及他離開星球和旅途上的事。這是從他的談話中逐漸累積訊息而得知的，就這樣，在第三天時，我聽到了有關猢猻麵包樹可能造成的災難。

這一次，還是得感謝那隻綿羊，因為牠的緣故，小王子突然憂心忡忡問我：「綿羊吃矮小的灌木，這是真的嗎？」

「是真的。」

「耶！我太高興了！」

我不明白羊吃灌木這件事有何重要。

小王子接著又問：「這麼說來，綿羊也吃猢猻麵包樹了囉？」

我對小王子說，猢猻麵包樹不是小灌木，而是可以長得和教堂一樣高的樹木，就算他帶一群大象回去，也吃不完一棵猢猻麵包樹。

提到一群大象，小王子笑了起來。

他說：「那可得把牠們一隻隻疊起來了。」

p. 38–39 不過，他又很有見地地説道：「猢猻麵包樹在長大之前，一開始時也是很小的吧？」

「沒錯！可是，你為什麼要綿羊去吃小猢猻麵包樹呢？」

他答道：「唉！這還用説嘛！」他説得一副事情是顯而易見的樣子，我只得自己努力去猜想可能的答案。

原來，小王子的星球就像所有的星球一樣，都同時長著有益和有害的植物。好的種子會生出好的植物，不好的種子會生出不好的植物。然而，種子是看不到的。

種子沈睡在泥土裡，直到其中一粒種子想甦醒過來，於是種子會開始舒展自己，起初會有點靦腆地開始把可愛無辜的小嫩枝向上朝著太陽生長。

如果它是蘿蔔的幼苗或是玫瑰花的嫩芽，就任由它生長；而如果它是有害的植物，一看到它就要把它拔掉。現在，在小王子家鄉的星球上，有一些可怕的種子——就是猢猻麵包樹的種子。星球上的土壤裡有很多種不一樣的種子，如果太晚發現發芽的是一株猢猻麵包樹，那就無法把它拔除了，它會盤踞整顆星球。

p. 40–41 猢猻麵包樹的樹根更會穿過星球，如果星球太小、猢猻麵包樹太多的話，樹根就會把星球撐裂而成碎塊。

「這是紀律問題。」後來小王子對我説：「當你早晨漱洗完畢後，要立即小心照料你的星球。你必須按時去拔猢猻麵包樹的幼苗，它們和玫瑰花的幼苗長得很像，一發現它們，就要立刻把它拔除。這個工作很乏味，不過很容易做。」

有一天，小王子勸我用心畫一幅漂亮的畫，讓我家鄉的小孩子們能有一個深刻的印象。

「要是有一天他們去旅行，那會對他們很有用的。」他對我說：「有時候，把今天的工作延個幾天並不妨礙，但如果是猢猻麵包樹這種事，那就會造成災難。我知道有一個星球，住著一位懶惰鬼，他曾經疏忽了三棵小灌木……」

p. 42 因此，在小王子向我描述的時候，我便把那個星球畫了下來。我不太喜歡以道德家的口吻說話，但猢猻麵包樹的危險性鮮為人知，這對住在小行星上的人來說是非常危險的，所以這一次我打破緘默，說道：「孩子們，要注意猢猻麵包樹啊！」

為了警惕我的朋友們——他們和我一樣都未曾察覺到這種危險——我花了很大的工夫畫了這張圖。提出這種警告，費點力氣是值得的。

或許你會問：「為什麼在這本書裡，其他的圖畫都不像猢猻麵包樹這幅這麼大呢？」其實答案很簡單，我也試著想畫小一點，卻克制不了，當我在畫猢猻麵包樹時，心情是特別激切的。

6

p. 44–45 啊！小王子！我逐漸明白了你帶著點憂傷的生活了。長久以來，你唯一的消遣就是欣賞夕陽的景色。我是在第四天的早晨才得知這一點的，當時你對我說：「我很喜歡看夕陽，我們現在去看一回夕陽吧……」

「但我們得等一下。」我說。

「等？等什麼？」

「等太陽下山呀！」

起初你好像很驚訝，隨即笑了笑。你說：「我以為我是在自己的家鄉呢！」

的確，大家都知道，當美國正中午的時候，法國正好是日落時分。假如你能在一分鐘之內飛到法國，就可以看到夕陽，只可惜法國太遠了。但是，在你的小星球上，你只需要把椅子移動幾步就行了。只要你想看夕陽，隨時都可以看到。

「我有一天曾經看過四十四次的日落呢！」過了一會，你又說：「你知道的，人在傷心時，特別喜歡夕陽……」

「這麼說來，在你看了四十四次夕陽的那一天，你很傷心嗎？」

然而，小王子沒有回答。

7

p. 46–47 第五天，又因為綿羊的緣故，我得知了小王子生活裡的另一個秘密。小王子一副好像默默思索很久得到什麼想法似地，突然沒頭沒腦地問我：「一隻羊如果吃小灌木的話，那牠是否也吃花呢？」

「羊吃任何搆得到的東西。」我說。

「即使是有刺的花也吃嗎？」

「沒錯，有刺的花牠也吃。」

「那麼，這些刺有什麼用處呢？」

我不知道怎樣回答。當時我正忙著要把一枚卡死在引擎內的螺絲釘擰鬆，我很擔心，我發現飛機故障得很嚴重，更讓我著急的是水也快喝完了。

「這些刺有什麼用處呢？」小王子一旦問問題，總是要得到答案。我當時正與那枚螺絲釘陷入苦戰，於是未經思索便回答了他：「那些刺一點用處也沒有，它之所以長刺，是因為它很惡毒。」

「噢！」沈默片刻之後，小王子口氣不滿地說：「我不相信！花很柔弱，很單純，它們儘可能讓自己安心，以為長刺就可以讓它們看起來很厲害……」

p. 48–49 我沒有回答。此刻我在想：「如果再轉不動這顆螺絲釘，我就要用鐵鎚把它敲下來。」小王子又打斷我的思緒。

「你真的認為花⋯⋯」

「哦，不，我沒在想什麼，我只是隨口回答你的問題，我還有正事要忙！」

他很吃驚地望著我。

「是正事！」

他看著我，我拿著鐵鎚，手指沾滿油污，身體伏在一個他覺得很醜陋的東西上。

「你說話就跟那些大人一樣！」

這話讓我有點慚愧。他接著又毫不客氣地說道：「你什麼事都搞糊塗了⋯⋯你把事情都混在一塊兒了！」他著實生氣了起來，金黃色的頭髮在微風中顫動著。「我知道有一個星球，上面住著一位滿臉通紅的先生。他從來沒聞過花香、看過星星。他沒有愛過任何人，在他一生當中，除了算帳，他沒做過任何其他的事。他和你一樣，整天就說著：『我是一個有正事要幹的人！』而這讓他覺得非常驕傲，其實他簡直不算是個人——他是一個蘑菇！」

p. 50–51 「一個什麼？」

「一個蘑菇！」這時小王子氣得臉都白了。「花長刺已經有幾百萬年了，羊吃花也有幾百萬年了，去了解花為何要辛辛苦苦地長那些毫無用處的刺，難道不是正事嗎？羊與花之間的戰爭不重要嗎？難道這不會比一位紅臉胖子的帳目來得重要嗎？」

「假如我知道我的星球上長著一朵全世界獨一無二的花，有一天早晨，卻被一隻小綿羊在無意中一口吃了，難道這不重要嗎？」

他的臉漸漸變紅，繼續說著：「如果有一個人很喜歡一朵花，而那朵花在千千萬萬的星星中是獨一無二的，那當他看著星星時，他就會感到很滿足。他可以對自己說：『我的花就在某一顆星星上面……』但是，如果有一隻綿羊把花給吃了，那麼對那個人來說，剎那間，所有的星星都會消失的。難道這不重要嗎？」

p. 52 小王子無法再說下去，他突然哭了起來。夜幕已垂，我丟下手中的工具。此刻，我的鐵鎚、螺絲釘、口渴和死亡，又有什麼要緊呢？在某顆星，某個星球——我的星球，地球上——有位小王子正需要人安慰。我把他摟入懷中，輕輕地搖著，並對他說：「你鍾愛的花不會有危險，我會幫你的綿羊畫一個口罩，在你的花周圍畫一道欄杆。我會……」

我真的不知道該對他說些什麼。我感到自己很笨拙，我不知道如何才能觸及他，去哪裡找到……。淚鄉，是一個如此神秘的國度。

8

p. 53 很快地，我對這朵花便有了更深的瞭解。在小王子星球上的花都很單純，它們只有一層花瓣，不佔空間也不打擾人。早晨它們在草叢裡綻放，晚上時便凋落。

但是，有一天，不知從哪裡飄來的一粒種子，冒出了新芽，小王子非常密切地觀察這株幼苗，發現它跟其他的幼苗長得不一樣。這很有可能是猢猻麵包樹的新品種。可是過沒多久，這株灌木便停止生長，並且即將開花。

p. 54–55 小王子看到它長出了一個大花苞，總覺得它會開出很神奇的東西出來。但這朵花兒繼續躲在綠萼裡，精心打扮自己。她仔細心地挑選顏色，慢慢地妝扮自己，一片一片地整理著花瓣。她不希望像田裡的罌粟花一樣，縐巴巴地來到這個世界。她要在最豔麗照人的時刻出現。啊！是的，她很虛榮！她神秘兮兮了好幾天，然後，有一天早晨，就在太陽昇起的時候，她忽然亮相了。

在所有這些辛勤的裝扮工作之後，她打著哈欠說道：「噯！我還沒完全清醒過來呢……真不好意思，我的花瓣還沒梳整好……」

但是小王子已經禁不住地讚嘆：「妳好美呀！」

「是嗎？」她溫柔地回答說：「我還是和太陽同時出生的呢……」

小王子看得出來她不懂得謙虛，不過，她是那麼的令人讚嘆！

「我想該吃早餐了。」她緊接著說道：「你會體貼地對待我嗎？」

小王子很尷尬地趕緊去找了一個裝滿清水的灑水器。於是，他便一直照顧著這朵花。

p. 56–57 不久後，她也開始用她的虛榮心來折磨小王子。好比說，有一天，在她提到她的四根刺時，她對小王子說：「有著利爪的老虎們，來吧！」

「在我的星球上沒有老虎。」小王子反駁道：「而且，老虎是不吃雜草的。」

「我不是雜草。」那朵花溫柔地答道。

「對不起……」

「我一點也不怕老虎。」她繼續說道：「但是我怕吹風，我想你沒有幫我準備屏風吧？」

「怕吹風……對一株植物來說是很不幸的。」小王子評論道，接著自言自語說：「這朵花真不太好侍候……」

「晚上的時候，你要用玻璃罩把我罩住，你住的地方太冷了，很不舒服。我原來住的那個地方……」說到這裡，她就自己打住了。她來到這裡的時候還是一顆種子，不可能知道任何其他世界的事情。

為了避免自己天真的謊言被抓到把柄，她困窘地以幾聲咳嗽來掩飾，好把過錯都推到小王子的身上。「屏風呢？」

p. 58–59 「我正要去找的時候，你叫住我了！」

這時，她又強迫自己多咳了幾聲，好讓小王子覺得良心不安。

儘管小王子真心誠意地喜歡她，但也很快就對她產生懷疑了。他把她那些無關緊要的話看得太認真了，而這讓他很不快樂。

「我實在不應該聽她的話。」有一天他向我傾訴：「人永遠不要去聽信花的話，只要單純地欣賞他們，聞聞他們的花香就好。我那朵花讓我的星球到處花香四溢，但是我卻不知道如何享受它。那個老虎利爪的故事，原本該讓我對她充滿憐惜的，但是卻讓我很生氣……」

他接著吐露道：「當時我什麼都不懂！我應該從她的行為而不是言語來作判斷的。她在我的星球上散發芳香，照亮我的生命，我實在不應該離她而去！我應該看出她那些愚蠢偽裝下的溫柔。花都是很矛盾的！可惜我那時候太年輕，不知道怎麼去愛她。」

9

p. 60–61 我想，他是趁著一群野生候鳥遷移時離開的。在臨走的那天早晨，他把他的星球整理了一番。他仔細地清理了活火山。他擁有兩座活火山，在早晨用來熱早餐非常方便。

另外，他還有一座死火山，不過正如他所說的：「世事難料！」

所以，他也很仔細地把死火山清理乾淨。如果清理乾淨，火山就不會突然爆發，而只會慢慢地、穩定地燃燒。火山爆發就好像煙囪裡起火一樣。

當然，我們地球上的人因為很小，沒辦法清理地球上的火山，所以火山給人帶來了很多麻煩。

小王子有些感傷地把最後的一些猢猻麵包樹幼苗拔除。他想自己將一去不回，所以在這最後一天的早晨，那些熟悉的工作讓他備感珍貴。當他幫那朵花澆最後一次水，並準備為她罩上玻璃罩的時候，他的眼淚幾乎要奪眶而出。

「再見了！」他對那朵花說。但花沒有回答。

「再見！」他又說了一次。

那花咳了起來，但不是因為感冒的緣故。

p. 62–63 「我以前很傻。」最後，她對他說：「請你原諒我，希望你能快樂起來。」

他很驚訝花對他沒有任何責備的話，他舉著玻璃罩，站在那裡不知手措，他對花這種恬靜的溫柔感到很不習慣。

「我當然是愛你的，你卻一直都不知道。」花對他說：「我想這都該怪我，但這都不重要了。不過你竟和我一樣的傻。讓自己快樂起來……。把玻璃罩放下吧，我已經不需要了。」

「可是，風……」

「我的感冒沒有那麼嚴重……，夜晚的空氣對我有益。別忘了，我是一朵花。」

「可是，動物……」

「如果我想認識蝴蝶，總得先忍受幾隻毛毛蟲呀！聽說蝴蝶很漂亮，況且除了蝴蝶和毛毛蟲外，還有誰會來看我？你就要遠行了。至於大動物，我一點也不怕牠們，我有利爪。」她很天真地展示了她的四根刺。

然後，她說：「別這麼依依不捨，這樣很令人難受。既然決定要離開，現在就走吧！」

她不想讓小王子看到她哭泣。

因為，她是一朵如此驕傲的花……

10

p. 65 小王子發現自己身在第 325、326、327、328、329 和 330 號小行星附近，因此便先開始拜訪這些小行星，以便增長見聞。

第一個小行星上面住著一位國王，他身穿高貴的紫袍貂皮大衣，坐在一張簡單但很有威嚴的寶座上。

「啊！有一位臣民來了。」當國王看到小王子的時候叫道。

小王子心想：「他以前從來沒見過我，怎麼會認得我是他的臣民呢？」小王子不曉得，這個世界對國王來說是很單純的——除了國王自己以外，所有的人都是他的臣民。

p. 66–67 「走近一點，好讓我可以看清楚些。」國王說道。他感到非常驕傲，因為終於有人被他統治了。

小王子四處瞧著，想找個地方坐下來，但整個星球都被國王華麗的貂皮大衣給遮蓋了，所以他只好站著。但他因為很累了，便打起呵欠來。

「在君王面前打呵欠是不合禮法的。」國王說道：「我禁止你打呵欠。」

「我忍不住。」小王子困窘地答道：「我剛長途跋涉而來，還沒有好好休息……」

「這樣的話，那我命令你打呵欠」國王說：「我已經有很多年沒看到人打呵欠了。打呵欠對我來說，是件很新鮮的事。來吧！再打呵欠吧！這是命令。」

「這倒讓我緊張了……，我打不出呵欠來了……」小王子紅著臉說。

p. 68–69 「好吧！好吧！」國王答道：「那麼……我命令你一會兒打呵欠，一會兒……」他有點結巴，顯得不耐煩。

國王所堅持的是他的權威要受到尊重，不容許有人違抗。他是一個獨裁君王，但因為他心地善良，所以下達的命令都很合理。

他常說道：「要是我命令一位將軍把自己變成一隻海鳥，而這位將軍沒有遵從我的命令，那並不是這位將軍的錯，而是我的錯。」

「我可以坐下嗎？」小王子有些膽怯地問道。

「我命令你坐下。」國王回答著，一面很有威嚴地挪了一下他的貂皮大衣。

小王子覺得很好奇，這個星球那麼小，國王能統治些什麼呢？「陛下。」他對國王說：「請容許我問您一個問題……」

「我命令你發問。」國王很快地說道。

「陛下……您統治些什麼呢？」

「統治一切。」國王簡潔地說。

「統治一切？」

國王作了一個手勢，指著他的星球、其他的星球和所有的星星。

「全部都是？」小王子問。

p. 70–71 「全部都是……」國王答道。

原來因為他不只是獨裁者，還是全宇宙的獨裁者。

「這些星星會聽從你的命令嗎？」

「當然。」國王說：「它們會馬上遵從，我不允許有人抗命。」

這樣的權力令小王子讚嘆不已。假如他能擁有這麼大的權力，那他在一天之內，就可以欣賞到不只四十四次的夕陽，而是七十二次，或一百次，甚至二百次，而且不必移動他的椅子！這時他想起了那顆被他遺棄的小星球，他感到有點悲傷，於是他鼓起勇氣請求國王幫忙：「我想看夕陽……請您幫我……命令太陽下山……」

「如果我命令一位將軍像隻蝴蝶一樣，從一朵花飛到另一朵花，或寫一齣悲劇，或是把自己變成一隻海鳥，要是這位將軍沒有執行所接到的命令，那麼，你說，我們兩個是誰錯了呢？是將軍，還是我自己？」

「是你不對。」小王子很確定地說道。

「完全正確。我們只能要求別人去做他能夠履行的任務。」國王繼續道：「會被人接受的權威，首先要建立在合理的基礎上。如果你命令你的子民去投海，他們一定會起義革命。我有權力要求服從，那也是因為我的命令很合理。」

「那麼我的夕陽呢？」小王子追問道。他一旦提出問題，就會追問到底。

p. 72–73 「你會看到你要的夕陽的，我會下命令的。不過，根據我的統治方法，我必須等到有利的時機。」

「什麼時候才是有利的時機？」小王子問道。

「這個嘛！」國王答著，在回答之前，他翻閱了一本厚厚的曆書。

「是這樣的！那大概……大概……是在今天晚上七點四十分左右，你會看到我的命令被確實執行！」

小王子打起呵欠來，有點遺憾看不到夕陽。而且，現在他已經開始覺得無聊了。「我在這裡沒有什麼事情可做。」他對國王說：「我應該啟程了。」

「不要走。」國王說，他非常得意終於有個臣民。「不要走，我任命你當部長！」

「什麼部長？」

「司……司法部長！」

「可是這裡沒有人可以審判呀！」

「這很難說。」國王對他說：「我尚未巡視過這個星球的所有領土。我太老了，這裡又太小，沒有地方可以駕馬車，走路又太累人。」

「哦，我都巡視過了！」小王子說著，轉身向這個星球的另一頭再看了一眼。「那裡就跟這裡一樣，一個人也沒有……」

「那麼，你就審判你自己吧。」國王回答，「這是最困難的事情。審判自己要比審判別人困難得多，如果你能正直地審判自己，那麼，你就是一位真正的智者。」

p. 74–75 小王子說：「沒錯，但我在任何地方都可以審判自己，不需要住在這個星球上。」

「這個嘛！」國王說：「我有充分的理由相信，在我星球上的某個地方有一隻很老的老鼠，在晚上可以聽到牠的聲音。你可以審判牠，並不時地判牠死刑。這樣，牠能否活命就全看你的審判，可是你每次判刑後都得赦免牠，因為我們只有這隻老鼠了。」

「我不喜歡判任何人死刑。」小王子說道：「而且，我該走了。」

「不要走。」國王說。

小王子準備好要啟程，但又不想讓這位老國王傷心。「如果陛下希望命令被立即奉行。」他說：「就給我下一道合理的命令吧，譬如說，命令我在一分鐘之內離開。在我看來，現在正是有利的時機……」

國王沒有回答，小王子猶豫了一會，嘆了口氣，便要離開。

「我任命你當大使。」國王急忙喊道，擺出一副威嚴的模樣。

「大人就是這麼奇怪。」小王子自言自語地啟程離開。

11

p. 76–77 第二個星球上住著一位虛榮的人。

「啊！有我的崇拜者來訪了！」當他看到小王子前來時，老遠就叫了起來。對虛榮的人來說，所有的人都是他的崇拜者。

「嗨。」小王子說：「你戴的帽子好古怪。」

「這是用來答禮的。」虛榮的人答道：「可惜的是，從來沒有人經過這裡。」

「是嗎？」小王子說，他不瞭解這位虛榮的人所說的話。

「鼓掌！」虛榮的人命令道。

小王子鼓起掌來，虛榮的人便舉起他的帽子答禮。「這比拜訪國王要有趣多了。」小王子自言自語道，然後又拍起手來，虛榮的人也再次舉帽答禮。

經過五分鐘的重複動作之後，小王子開始厭倦了這種單調的遊戲。「要怎麼做你才會把帽子放下來呢？」他問道。

可是虛榮的人沒有聽到他的話。一個虛榮的人除了讚美的話，什麼也聽不見。

p. 78 「你真的很崇拜我嗎？」他問小王子。

「你說的『崇拜』——是什麼意思？」

「崇拜的意思就是，你認為我是這個星球上最英俊、衣著最好、最富有、最聰明的人。」

「可是，在這個星球上就只有你一個人呀！」

「就當作是做好事，你還是一樣地崇拜我吧。」

「我崇拜你。」小王子說著，輕輕地聳了聳肩膀。「不過，這種事為什麼會讓令你這麼感興趣？」小王子說罷便離開了。

「大人們實在非常奇怪。」小王子繼續踏上旅程，自言自語地說著。

12

p. 79 下一個星球住著一位酒鬼。這次的拜訪很短暫，但是卻讓小王子感到很無奈。

「你在那裡做什麼？」他問酒鬼。他看他酒鬼一個人默默地坐在一堆空瓶子和裝滿酒的瓶子前面。

「在喝酒。」酒鬼神情陰鬱地答道。

p. 80 「你為什麼要喝酒？」小王子問。

「為了遺忘。」酒鬼回答。

「遺忘什麼？」小王子問道，心裡頭為他感到難過。

「忘掉我的羞恥。」酒鬼低下頭來，坦承道。

「什麼羞恥？」小王子追問道，想幫助他。

「喝酒的羞恥！」酒鬼說罷就不再說話。小王子於是困惑不解地離開了。

「大人真的是非常非常的奇怪。」他自言自語著，又繼續啟程了。

13

p. 81 第四個星球屬於一個商人所有。這個商人忙得不可開交，所以小王子到達的時候，他甚至連頭也沒抬起來。

「你好。」小王子對他說：「你的香菸已經熄了。」

「三加二等於五。五加七等於十二。十二加三等於十五。你好。十五加七等於二十二。二十二加六等於二十八。我沒有空再把它點燃。二十六加五等於三十一。哇！總共是五億零一百六十二萬二千七百三十一。」

「五億個什麼？」小王子問。

p. 82「噫？你還在那裡啊？五億零一百萬……我不記得了……我有很多工作要做！我有的是正經事要幹，沒有閒工夫理會芝麻小事。二加五等於七……」

「五億零一百萬個什麼？」小王子重複問道。他只要提出問題，就會追問到底。

商人抬起頭來。「我住在這個星球住了五十四年，當中，我只被打擾過三次。第一次是在二十二年前，當時不知道從哪裡來的一隻甲蟲掉到我的桌上，牠的聲音很吵，害我的計算錯了四次。第二次是在十一年前，那時我的風濕病發作，因為我的運動量不夠。我沒有時間鬼混，我有正事要處理。第三次……嗯，就是現在了！我剛剛是在說五億零一百萬……」

「一百萬個什麼？」

p. 84–85 商人突然瞭解到，如果沒有回答這個問題，他是沒有辦法得到安靜的。

「就是你有時可以在天空中看到的東西。」

「蒼蠅嗎？」

「喔！不對。小小的會發亮的東西。」

「蜜蜂？」

「不是！小小的金黃色的，會讓懶人幻想的東西。至於我，我是有正事要做的人，沒有時間去做白日夢。」

「啊！你說的是星星？」

「沒錯，就是星星。」

「那你要五億顆星星做什麼呢？」

「五億零一百六十二萬二千七百三十一顆。我是有正事要做的人，而且我做事很準確。」

「你要這些星星做什麼？」

「我要它們做什麼？」

「是啊！」

「不做什麼。我擁有它們。」

「你擁有這些星星？」

「沒錯。」

「可是，我曾經遇到一個國王，他……」

「國王不是擁有，他們是統治。這是很不一樣的。」

「擁有星星對你有什麼好處呢？」

「可以讓我變得很富有。」

「富有對你有什麼好處呢？」

「這樣我就可以買更多的星星，假如有新的星星被發現的話。」

p. 86–87 小王子自言自語著，「這種理由有點像那可憐的酒鬼……」雖然如此，小王子還想問下去：「一個人怎麼可能擁有星星呢？」

「不然，它們星星要屬於誰呢？」商人微慍地反問道。

「我不知道。不屬於任何人吧！」

「那麼，它們就是屬於我，因為我是第一個想到的人。」

「這就夠了嗎？」

「當然。如果你發現一顆不屬於任何人的鑽石，那它就屬於你。如果你發現一座不屬於任何人的島嶼，那島就是你的了。如果你比別人先想到一個主意，並取得專利，那它就專屬於你。所以，我擁有這些星星，因為沒有人比我更早想到要擁有它們。」

「不錯，這倒是真的。」小王子說：「那你要它們做什麼呢？」

「我管理它們，我把它們一數再數。」商人答道：「這事很困難，但我喜歡做正經事！」

小王子仍不滿意這個答案。「如果我擁有一條圍巾，我可以把它圍在脖子上帶走。如果我擁有一朵花，我可以把它摘下來帶走。可是，你沒辦法從天上把星星摘下來！」

「沒錯，但是我可以把它們存在銀行裡。」

「那是什麼意思？」

「就是說，我把星星的數目寫在一張小紙條上，然後在把紙條鎖在抽屜裡。」

「就這樣？」

「這樣就夠了！」商人說。

p. 88 「這很有趣。」小王子想道：「而且很有想像力，可是卻不重要。」對於什麼才是重要的事情，小王子的看法跟大人很不一樣。

「我自己擁有一朵花。」他繼續和商人說道：「我每天幫她澆水。我有三座火山，我每個星期都會把它們清理乾淨，我也清理那座死火山，因為誰也不知道它何時會爆發。我這樣擁有我的火山和花，對它們是有益處的，可是你對星星毫無益處。」

商人張大嘴巴，卻無言以對。於是，小王子便離開了。

「大人們實在太奇怪了。」他自言自語著，繼續踏上旅程。

14

p. 89 第五個星球非常奇特。它是所有的行星中最小的一個，它的大小只能容下一盞路燈和一位燈伕。小王子想不通：在天空中一個沒有人住，甚至連一間房子也沒有的星球上，要一盞路燈和一個燈伕有什麼用處。

儘管如此，但小王子仍暗自想道：「這個人看起來是很荒謬，然而跟國王、自負的人、商人和酒鬼比起來，他還算好多了。

至少，他的工作比較有意義。當他點燃路燈時，就好像讓一顆星星或一朵花甦醒過來；當他熄燈時，就好像送這朵花或是星星進入夢鄉。這是一件美好的工作。既然很美好，也就真的有用了。」

p. 90 抵達這顆星球的時候，他非常恭敬地向燈伕敬禮。

「早安。你剛剛為什麼要熄燈呢？」

「這是職責。」燈伕答道：「早安。」

「是什麼樣的職責？」

「就是規定我要熄燈。晚安。」燈伕又把路燈點燃。

「可是你剛剛為什麼又把它點燃呢？」

「這是職責。」燈伕回答。

「我不懂。」小王子說。

「不需要懂。」燈伕說：「職責就是職責。早安。」

他又把燈熄了，然後拿起一條有紅方格子紋路的手帕來擦額頭。

p. 92–93 「我從事的職業很辛苦。以前還說得過去，早上熄燈，晚上點燈，白天剩餘的時間我可以處理私事，晚上剩餘的時間我可以睡覺。」

「在那之後呢？職責改變了嗎？」

「職責沒有改。」燈伕說道：「問題就在這裡！這個星球旋轉得一年比一年快，可是職責卻從未更改！」

「你是指？」小王子問。

「我是說這個星球每分鐘就旋轉一圈，我連休息片刻的時間都沒有。我每一分鐘內，就要點一次燈和熄一次燈。」

「那太好玩了！在你住的這個星球，一天只有一分鐘長！」

「這一點也不好玩！」燈伕說：「在我們聊天的這段時間，已經一個月過去了。」

「一個月？」

「沒錯，已經過了三十分鐘，也就是三十天了！晚安。」他又把燈點亮。

小王子望著他，他很喜歡這個盡忠職守的燈伕。他想起了他以前只要挪動一下椅子就可以看到夕陽，他想幫助這一位朋友。

p. 94–95 小王子說：「這個嘛，我可以告訴你一個隨時都可以休息的方法。」

「我一直都想休息。」燈伕說。人要既忠實又可以偷懶，是有可能的事。

小王子繼續解釋道：「你的星球那麼很小，你只要走三步就可以繞一周。所以，你只要慢慢地走，就可以一直置身在陽光底下。當你想休息時，就只要這樣走幾步……那麼，你想要白天有多長，它就可以有多長。」

「那對我沒有什麼好處。」燈伕說：「我生平最喜歡的事，就是睡覺。」

「那麼你很不幸。」小王子說。

「我是很不幸。」燈伕說道：「早安。」然後他又把燈熄滅。

小王子繼續啟程時，他自言自語道：「這個人一定會被其他的人嘲笑，像國王、自負的人、酒鬼和商人。雖然如此，在他們之中，他是我唯一不會覺得荒謬的人。或許，那是因為他心裡頭想的不是自己的事。」他惋惜地嘆了口氣，又說道：「在他們之中，這個人是我唯一可以交成朋友的人，可是他的星球實在太小了，容納不下兩個人……」

其實，小王子不敢承認，離開這個星球讓他最感到遺憾的事，是在那裡每天可以看到一千四百四十次的日落！

15

p. 96–97 第六個星球比上一個星球大了十倍。上面住著一位寫了很多大部頭書的老先生。

「啊！你看！來了一位探險家！」當他看到小王子到來的時候叫道。小王子坐在桌子上，有些氣喘吁吁。他已經旅行很久，也很遠了！

「你從哪裡來呀？」老先生問他說。

「那本厚重的書是什麼？」小王子問，「你在做什麼呢？」

「我是個地理學家。」老先生答道。

「什麼是地理學家？」小王子問。

「地理學家就是一位知道所有海洋、河流、城鎮、山脈和沙漠的位置的學者。」

「那真有意思。」小王子說道：「終於有一位有真正職業的人了！」他四處環顧地理學家的星球，這是他所見過最富麗堂皇的星球。

「你的星球真漂亮。」他說：「這裡有海洋嗎？」

「我不清楚。」地理學家說。

「啊！」小王子很失望。「那，這裡有高山嗎？」

「我不清楚。」地理學家說。

「有城鎮、河川和沙漠嗎？」

「這個我也不清楚。」地理學家答道。

p. 98–99「可是，你是一個地理學家呀！」

「沒錯。」地理學家說：「但我不是個探險家。在我的星球上，連一個探險家也沒有。地理學家的工作不是出外去記錄城鎮、河流、山脈、海、大洋和沙漠的。地理學家太重要了，不能出去閒逛浪費時間。他不會離開他的書桌，可是他會在書房裡接見探險家們。他會向他們提出問題，並把他們旅途中的見聞記錄下來。如果其中某個見聞引人關注，地理學家就會調查這位探險家的品性。」

「為什麼要調查？」

「因為探險家如果說謊，會給地理學家的書帶來很大的災禍。還有，一個探險家如果酒喝太多的話也會這樣。」

「為什麼？」小王子問道。

「喝醉酒的人會把一個看成兩個，讓地理學家誤把只有一座山的地方，記錄為兩座山。」

p. 100–101「我認識一個人。」小王子說：「他可能會是個差勁的探險家。」

「那是可能的。接著，如果證明這個探險家的品性良好，便得下令調查他的發現。」

「去看一看嗎？」

「不是，那太麻煩了。我會要求探險家拿出證據。譬如說，如果他發現的是一座高山，那他就得從那裡帶回一些大石頭。」地理學家突然興奮起來：「你就是從遠方來的！你是一位探險家！你必須描述你的星球給我聽！」

地理學家隨即翻開他的大筆記本，削起鉛筆。他把探險家的敘述先以鉛筆記下，等到探險家提出證據後，再用墨水寫下。

「好了嗎？」地理學家充滿期待地說。

「啊，我住的地方，不是很有趣。」小王子說道：「它很小，我有三座火山，兩座活火山，另一座是死火山。不過，誰也不能確定它會不會再爆發。」

「的確沒有人可以確定。」地理學家說。

「我還有一朵花。」

「我們不記錄花。」地理學家說道。

「為什麼呢？這朵花是我的星球上最漂亮的一樣東西！」

「因為它們的生命是『稍縱即逝』的。」

「『稍縱即逝』是什麼意思？」

p. 102–103 地理學家說道：「地理學是最有價值的書，永遠不會過時。一座山的位置是不太可能會改變的，海洋裡的水乾涸的機率也是微乎其微。我們寫的都是永恆的東西。」

「但是，死火山是有可能再復活的。」小王子打岔道：「『稍縱即逝』是什麼意思？」

「不管是死火山或還是活火山，對我們來說都一樣。」地理學家說：「對我們來說，重要的是——山，它不會改變。」

「那『稍縱即逝』是什麼意思？」小王子重複問道。他是一旦提出問題就會問到底。

「意思是，『它有迅速消失的危險。』」

「我的花有迅速消失的危險嗎？」

「當然有了。」

「我的花是稍縱即逝的。」小王子喃喃自語道：「她只有四根刺可以防衛自己，對抗外界，而我卻把她孤伶伶地留在我的星球上！」

這是他第一次感到懊悔。不過，他又再度鼓起勇氣。「你會建議我現在到哪裡去探訪呢？」他問道。

「地球。」地理學家答道。「它的名聲不錯。」

於是，小王子離開了，心裡頭想著他的花。

16

p. 104–105 第七個星球，便是地球了。

地球可不是個普通的行星呢！算一算，在那裡有一百一十一位國王（當然，不要忘了，非洲土著的國王也包括在內），七千個地理學家，九十萬個商人，七百五十萬個酒鬼，三億一千一百萬個虛榮的人。也就是說，大約有二十億個大人。

為了讓你對地球的大小有個概念，我來告訴你，在電力還沒有發明以前，整個六大洲裡，共有四十六萬二千五百一十一個路燈燈伕。

遠遠地看過去，那景象還真是壯觀。這些路燈燈伕人的動作，就好像歌劇中的芭蕾舞者，極有規律地移動著。

首先登場的是紐西蘭和澳洲的燈伕，他們把路燈點亮後，便去休息睡覺。

其次，中國和西伯利亞的燈伕登場表演後，也退下進入邊廂。

接著，輪到蘇俄和印度燈伕，然後是非洲和歐洲，再來是南美洲、北美洲。他們登台的順序決不會弄錯，那場面實在了不起。

在北極只有一盞路燈，南極也是。唯有這兩個燈伕人可以輕鬆悠哉地度日：因為他們在一年中只需工作兩次。

17

p. 106 當一個人想賣弄才智時，難免會稍微偏離真相。在我告訴你們有關燈伕的事情時，我的話並不是那麼可靠。我知道我可能給那些不瞭解地球的人一個錯誤的概念。人在地球上所佔的地方很小。如果把地球上的二十億居民全部聚集靠攏，就像在開市民大會那樣，那他們可以很從容地一齊站在一個二十平方英里的廣場上。你可以把全部的人類聚集在一座太平洋中的小島上。

p. 108–109 當然，如果你這麼告訴大人，他們是不會相信的。大人們認為他們要佔有很大的地方，把自己想得像猢猻麵包樹那樣大得了不起。

你應該建議人們計算一下，人們那麼崇拜數字，這樣會讓他們很高興的。但是，別把你的時間浪費在這件額外的工作上，那沒有必要，相信我。

當小王子抵達地球時，他非常訝異，竟然沒看到半個人。當他看到沙地上有個銀色的圈圈在展開時，他開始擔心自己走錯星球。

「晚安。」小王子隨口說道。

「晚安。」蛇說。

「我來到的這個星球，是什麼星球呀？」小王子問。

「這是地球。這裡是非洲。」蛇答道。

「啊！那麼說，在地球上沒有人囉？」

「這裡是沙漠，沙漠裡沒有人。地球是很大的。」他說。

小王子坐在一顆石頭上，抬眼望著天空。「我在想，」他說：「星星發光，是不是要讓每一個人都能找到屬於自己的星星啊？

你看我的星球，它就在我們的頭頂上，只是它離得好遠啊！」

「它很美耶。」蛇說道：「你為什麼會來到地球呢？」

「我和一朵花處得不好。」小王子說。

「這樣啊！」蛇說。他們都沉默了下來。

p. 111 「哪裡有人呢？」小王子終於又繼續聊起話來：「在沙漠裡有點寂寞……」

「在人群中也會寂寞。」蛇說道。

小王子注視著他好一會。最後說道：「你是個有趣的動物，你細得像手指頭一樣……」

「我可是比一個國王的手指還要厲害的。」蛇說。

小王子笑道：「你不可能那麼厲害……你連腳都沒有，跑不遠的。」

「我可以送你到很遠的地方，比任何船可以載你去的地方都還要遠。」蛇說。他把自己纏繞在小王子的腳踝上，就像一只黃金鐲子。

p. 112 「任何被我碰到的人，我都會把他送回老家去。」蛇又說道：「不過你很天真，而且從來一顆遙遠的星星來到這……」

小王子沒有回答。

「我很同情你，你在這個堅硬的地球上，太脆弱了。」蛇說：「如果有一天，你很想念你的星球的話，我可以幫助你。我可以……」

「噢！我瞭解你的意思。」小王子說：「可是，為什麼你說話都好像在講謎語似的？」

「這些謎題我都能解得開。」蛇說。

之後兩人又沉默不語。

18

p. 113 小王子越過沙漠，看到一朵花。那朵花只有三片花瓣，很不起眼。

「早安。」小王子說。

「早安。」花說。

「人都在哪裡呢？」小王子很有禮貌地問道。

這朵花曾看見一個商隊經過。

「人？我想應該有六、七個人吧。幾年前我曾見過他們，可是沒有人知道在哪裡可以找到他們，風把他們吹走了。他們沒有長根，留不住。」

「再見。」小王子說。

「再見。」花說。

19

p. 114–115 在那之後，小王子爬上一座高山。以前他所認識的山，只有那三座高及膝蓋的火山，他還把那座死火山當凳子。他自言自語道：「從這麼高的山上，應該可以看到將整個星球和所有的人……」然而，除了許多鋒利的山峰外，他什麼也看不到。

「你好。」他說，以防漏看了什麼。

「你好……你好……你好……」回音答道。

「你是誰？」小王子說。

「你是誰……你是誰……你是誰……」回音答道。

「請你當我的朋友，我好寂寞。」他說。

「我好寂寞……我好寂寞……我好寂寞。」回音回答。

「好古怪的星球！」他想道：「一片乾燥，地面又尖又硬。

而且人們沒有想像力，只會重複別人對他們說的話……。在我的星球上，我有一朵花，她都會先開口說話……」

20

p. 116–117 在經過沙漠、岩石和雪地的長途跋涉之後，小王子終於找到了一條大路。所有的道路都會通向人們所在之地。

「早安。」他說。

他正站在一個玫瑰花盛開的花園前。

「早安。」玫瑰花們說。

小王子盯著她們瞧。她們看起來都跟他的花好像。

「你們是誰？」他非常驚訝地問道。

「我們是玫瑰花。」玫瑰花們說。

「噢！」小王子說。

他很難過。他的花曾告訴他，她是全宇宙中僅有的一朵花，然而光是在這座花園裡，就有五千朵長得和她一模一樣的花！

「她一定會很生氣，」他自言自語道：「她要是看到這些花，一定會很惱火的……，她一定會拼命地咳嗽，為了怕被人取笑，她還會假裝快要死掉了，而我也只好裝出一副細心照顧她的模樣，不然她會真的讓自己死去，好讓我感到羞愧。」

p. 118 接著他又想道：「我本以為我很富有，因為我有一朵獨一無二的花，結果她不過是一朵普通的玫瑰花罷了。一朵普通的玫瑰花、三座只有我膝蓋那麼高的火山，而且其中的一座可能永遠不會再爆發了，這一切都不足以讓我成為一位偉大的王子……」於是，他躺在草地上哭了起來。

21

p. 119 就在這個時候，狐狸出現了。

「早安。」狐狸說。

「早安。」小王子有禮貌地回答著，雖然他轉過身時什麼也沒瞧見。

「我在這裡。」那聲音說：「在蘋果樹下。」

「你是誰？」小王子問，同時說道：「你長得真漂亮。」

「我是一隻狐狸。」狐狸說。

「過來跟我一起玩吧。」小王子提議道：「我心裡很難過。」

「我不能跟你一起玩。」狐狸說：「還沒有被馴養。」

「哦！對不起。」小王子說。他想了一會兒後，又問道：「『馴養』是什麼意思？」

p. 120–121 「你一定不是住在這裡的人。」狐狸說。「你在找什麼呢？」

「我在找人。」小王子說：「『馴養』是什麼意思？」

狐狸說：「人們有槍，而且會去打獵，實在很討厭。他們也養雞，這是他們唯一有趣的事情。你在尋找雞嗎？」

「不是。」小王子說。「我在尋找朋友。『馴養』是什麼意思？」

「那是一種常常被忽略的行為，它的意思是建立關係。」

「建立關係？」

「是的。」狐狸說道：「在我來看，你不過是個小男孩，就跟其他成千上萬的小男孩沒什麼兩樣。我不需要你，你也不需要我。對你來說，我不過是隻狐狸，跟其他成千上萬的狐狸沒什麼不同。但是，如果你馴養我，那麼，我們就會彼此需要了。那麼，對我來說，你就是這個世上獨一無二的了。對你來說，我也會是獨一無二的……」

p. 122-123 「我開始有點瞭解了。」小王子說：「有一朵花⋯⋯，我想她曾經馴養過我⋯⋯」

「這有可能。」狐狸說：「在地球上無奇不有。」

「哦，不是在地球上！」小王子說。

狐狸似乎很好奇。「在別的星球上？」

「是的。」

「那個星球上有獵人嗎？」

「沒有。」

「那就有意思了！有雞嗎？」

「沒有。」

「天底下沒有十全十美的事。」狐狸嘆道。

不過，他很快又回到正題。「我的生活很單調。我獵雞吃，人們獵我。所有的雞都一個模樣，所有的人也是。因此，我感到有些厭煩了。但是，如果你馴養了我，我的人生就會充滿陽光。我就會辨認出一種與眾不同的腳步聲，別的腳步聲會讓我嚇得躲到地下，你的腳步聲卻會像音樂般地把我從洞穴裡喚出來。

然後你看！你看到下面那邊的麥田了嗎？我不吃麵包，小麥對我沒什麼用處，麥田對我一點意義也沒有，這真掃興。但是，你有金黃色的頭髮，所以當你馴養我以後，事情會變得很美好，因為麥田的顏色也是金黃色的，這會讓我想起你，而且我也會愛上風吹過麥田的聲音⋯⋯」

p. 124-125 狐狸沉默不語，注視著小王子好一段時間。「請⋯⋯馴養我吧！」他說。

「我是很願意的。」小王子答道：「可是，我的時間不多。我還要去認識朋友，去見識見識很多事情。」

「只有你馴服的東西，你才能夠了解。」狐狸說：「人們一向沒有太多的時間去認識什麼事。他們在商店裡買現成的東西，但商店裡沒有賣朋友，所以人也就沒有朋友。如果你想要一個朋友，就馴養我吧！」

「那我必須做些什麼呢？」小王子問。

「你必須很有耐心。」狐狸答道：「首先，你必須坐在草地上離稍遠的地方。我會用餘光瞄你，而你什麼話也不用說。語言是誤會的源頭。但是，你每天要坐得靠我更近一點……」

隔天，小王子回來了。

「你最好每次回來的時間都一樣。」狐狸說：「譬如你在下午四點回來，那麼，在三點的時候我就會開始高興了。時間越接近，我就越高興。到快四點的時候，我便開始會坐立不安，我會了解到幸福的代價是什麼！但是，如果你每次來的時間都不一樣，我就不知道要在什麼時間做好迎接你的心理準備……應當要有一些的儀式的。」

「什麼是『儀式』？」小王子問。

p. 127 「那些也是常常被忽略的行為。」狐狸說道：「它會讓某一天不同於別的日子，某個小時不同於別的時刻。例如，獵人們就有一個儀式。每個星期四，他們會跟村裡的女孩子們跳舞。因此，星期四對我來說，就是一個美好的日子，我可以一直散步到葡萄園去！但是，如果獵人隨時想跳就跳，那麼所有的日子就都沒什麼不同，而我也就不會有什麼假期了。」

就這樣，小王子馴養了狐狸。當分離的時刻到來時，狐狸說：「啊，我會哭的。」

「這是你自己的過錯。」小王子說：「我從未想過要傷害你，但是你要我馴養你……」

「是這樣沒錯。」狐狸說。

p. 128–129 「可是，現在你卻想哭！」小王子說道。

「是啊。」狐狸說。

「那麼，馴養對你一點好處也沒有！」

「當然有好處，就因為麥田的顏色！」狐狸說：「你再去看看那些玫瑰花吧，你就會明白你的那一朵玫瑰花是全世界獨一無二的。然後再回來跟我道別，我會送你一個秘密當作禮物。」

於是小王子再去看看那些玫瑰花。「妳們和我的玫瑰花一點也不像。妳們對我一點也不具意義。」他告訴她們說：「沒有人馴養過妳們，妳們也未曾馴養過任何人。妳們就像我初次見到的那隻狐狸一樣，他不過就是成千上萬隻狐狸中的一隻。但是我和他做了朋友，因此現在他是全世界獨一無二的了。」

那些玫瑰花們覺得很沒面子。

「妳們是很美，不過也很空虛。」他繼續說道：「沒有人會為妳們而死。當然，一般的路人會認為我的玫瑰花和妳們沒什麼兩樣，但對我而言，她一朵就勝過妳們全部的花加起來。因為，我曾為她澆水，把她放在玻璃罩下，用屏風為她遮風避雨，為她除去毛毛蟲（只留下兩三隻來變成蝴蝶），聽她發牢騷或吹牛，或聆聽她的沉默不語。因為，她是『我的』玫瑰花。」

之後，他又回到狐狸那裡。

「再見。」他說道。

「再見。」狐狸說道：「這就是我的秘密，一個很簡單的秘密：一個人只有用心靈才能看得清楚，重要的東西是肉眼看不見的。」

p. 130 「重要的東西是肉眼看不見的。」小王子重複地說道，希望能把它牢牢記住。

「你在你的玫瑰花身上花的時間，讓她變得那麼重要。」

「我在我的玫瑰花身上所花的時間……」小王子重複唸道，好確定已經記下了。

「人們早已忘了這個真理，但是你不可以忘記。」狐狸說道：「你要為你所馴養的東西負責，你要永遠為你的玫瑰花負責……」狐狸說。

「我要為我的玫瑰花負責。」小王子重複道，以確定他已經記下了。

22

p. 131 「早安。」小王子說。

「早安。」鐵路的扳閘員說。

「你在這裡做什麼？」小王子問道。

「我把旅客分類，一千個人一批。」扳閘員說：「然後把載運他們的火車發車出去，有時往右，有時往左。」

一列燈火通明的快車，像雷鳴般轟隆地急馳而過，把扳閘員的小屋震得吱嘎響。

「他們好匆忙。」小王子說：「他們在找什麼呢？」

「就連火車司機自己也不知道。」扳閘員說。又有一列燈火通明的快車，往相反的方向轟隆隆地急馳而過。

「他們已經回來了嗎？」小王子問道。

「這不是剛剛的那些人。」扳閘員說：「這是對開列車。」

「他們不滿意原來的地方嗎？」小王子問。

p. 132 「沒有人會滿足於自己原來的地方的。」扳閘員說。

他們又聽到第三列燈火明亮的快車狂嘯而過。

「他們在追趕第一批的旅客嗎？」小王子問。

「他們沒有在追趕什麼。」扳閘員說：「他們在裡面睡覺，如果沒有睡著，就是在打呵欠。只有小孩子們才會把鼻子靠在玻璃窗上往外看。」

「只有小孩子們才知道他們在尋找什麼。」小王子說。「他們把時間花在一隻碎布娃娃上，那隻娃娃對他們來說就變得重要；如果有人把娃娃從他們身邊拿走，他們就會哭……」

「他們很幸運。」扳閘員說。

23

p. 133 「早安。」小王子說。

「早安。」商人說。這是一位販售止渴藥丸的商人。只要一個星期服用一顆藥丸，你就不會感到口渴想喝東西了。

「你為什麼要賣那些藥丸？」小王子問。

「因為它們可以節省很多時間。」商人說：「專家們已經計算過，服用這種藥丸，你每個星期可以省下五十三分鐘。」

「省下的五十三分鐘，要做些什麼呢？」

「做任何你想做的事。」

「假如我有五十三分鐘可以任意使用，」小王子自語道：「我會從容地走向一處清涼的泉水……」

24

p. 134–135 這是我的飛機在沙漠裡失事的第八天。當我聽著商人的故事時，我正好喝下水壺裡的最後一滴水。

我對小王子說：「啊，你這些往事很吸引人，可是我還沒有把飛機修理好，也沒有水可以喝了。如果我可以從容地走向一處清涼的泉水，我也會非常地高興！」

「我的狐狸朋友告訴我……」小王子對我說。

「我親愛的小朋友，這件事和狐狸扯不上關係呀！」

「為什麼沒有關係？」

「因為我們就快要渴死了。」

小王子並沒有聽懂我的話，因為他回答說：「即使快死了，能有個朋友也是件好事。譬如說，我就很高興能有狐狸這個朋友。」

「他不知道那種危機。」我自忖道：「他不會餓，不會渴，他只要一點點陽光就可以活了……」

但小王子凝視著我，回應我心裡的想法答道：「我也渴了……我們去找水井吧……」

我顯出厭煩的樣子。要在一望無際的沙漠中，漫無目的地找水井，實在荒謬。但儘管如此，我們還是出發了。

p. 136–137 當我們靜靜地跋涉幾個小時後，天黑了下來，星星開始露臉。我口渴得有點發燒，我看著星星，像是在做夢一樣。小王子之前所說的話在我腦海裡迴盪著。

「那你也會口渴囉？」我問道。

他沒有回答我的問題，只是對我說道：「水對於心靈也是有益的……」

我並不懂這些話的意思，不過我什麼也沒說……我很清楚，問他話是問不出什麼的。

他累了，便坐了下來。我坐在他的身旁。沉默了一會之後，他又說道：「這些星星真漂亮，因為有一朵人們看不到的花……」

我答道：「的確。」便不發一語，只靜靜地看著眼前在月光下的沙脊。

「沙漠很美。」小王子又說。

這倒是真的。我一直都很喜歡沙漠。坐在沙丘上，什麼也看不到，什麼也聽不見。然而，在一片靜寂之中，卻有個東西在閃耀，在吟唱……

小王子說：「讓沙漠變得美麗的，就是隱藏在某處的水井……」

我很驚訝，突然明白了沙子為何會發出神秘的光芒。小時候，我住在一棟老房子裡，傳說房子的下面埋有寶藏。

p. 138–139 當然，沒有人發現過這個寶藏，甚至也沒有人去尋寶過。但是，寶藏卻讓整個房子變得充滿魔力。在房子的心靈深處，埋藏了一個秘密……

「沒錯。」我對小王子說：「不論是房子、星星或沙漠，讓它們變美麗的都是肉眼看不到的東西！」

「我很高興。」他說：「你同意我的狐狸所說的話。」

當小王子睡著的時候，我把他抱入懷中，再度出發上路。我深受感動。我彷佛是懷著一件非常脆弱的珍寶，彷佛他是整個地球上最脆弱的東西了。

在月光下，我看著他蒼白的前額、緊閉的雙眼，以及在風中飄蕩的鬈髮。我心忖道：「我眼裡所看見的不過是副軀殼，而最重要東西，肉眼是看不見的……」

他微張的嘴唇微笑著。我不禁又想道：「這個熟睡中的小王子，讓我深受感動的，就是他對一朵花的忠誠，甚至在他睡著的時候，那朵玫瑰花的形像也在他心中照耀著，就像一盞燈的光輝一般……」於是，我覺得他變得更脆弱了。燈火需要被保護，不然一陣風吹來就會把它吹滅……

就這樣，我不停地走著，破曉時分，我終於找到了一口水井。

25

p. 140 小王子說:「人們坐著快車出發,卻不知道在尋找什麼。他們匆匆忙忙,不停地轉來轉去⋯⋯」他接著又說道:「這是沒必要的⋯⋯」

我們找到的這口井,不像撒哈拉沙漠裡的水井。撒哈拉沙漠裡的水井都是在沙地中挖個洞而已,但這口井卻像鄉村子裡的井,可是這裡沒有村莊,我還以為我是在作夢。

「真奇怪。」我對小王子說。「這個井什麼都有:轆轤、水桶、繩索⋯⋯」

他笑著,拉住繩子,轉動轆轤。轆轤像個被風遺忘已久的風向標,嘎吱作響。

p. 142–143 「你聽到了嗎?」小王子問:「我們喚醒了這座井,它正唱著歌。」

我不希望他因為拉繩子而把自己給累著了。「讓我來吧。」我說:「這對你來說太重了。」

我把水桶小心翼翼地拉放到井邊,我耳中響著轆轤的歌聲,看到晃動的水面上閃爍著陽光。

「我好想喝這些水。」小王子說:「給我一些水喝⋯⋯」

我這才瞭解他一直在尋找的是什麼東西!

我把水桶舉高到他的嘴邊。他閉上雙眼喝著水,彷彿在享用著盛宴似的。這些水不只是水而已。

這水是在星夜下走了許多路,在轆轤的歌唱中,在雙手的勞動之後才得到的。這水就像是一件對心靈有益的禮物。就好像在我小時候時,因為聖誕樹上的燈光、午夜彌撒的音樂、人們溫柔的笑臉,才使得聖誕禮物變得令人感到幸福。

「住在這裡的人們。」小王子說:「在一座花園裡栽種了五千朵玫瑰花⋯⋯卻無法從中找到他們想要尋找的東西⋯⋯」

「他們是找不到的。」我回答道。

「但他們所要尋找的東西，在一朵玫瑰花或一點兒水裡頭就可以找得到了……」

「沒錯，的確。」我說。

小王子又接著道：「眼睛是盲目的，人必須用心靈來看……」

p. 144–145 喝過水後，我的呼吸順暢多了。日出時，沙漠呈現出一片蜂蜜的顏色，這種顏色讓我心情愉快，可是我為何又有一種悲傷的感覺呢？

「你必須遵守你的諾言。」當小王子再次坐在我身旁時，他說道。

「什麼諾言？」

「你知道的……給我的綿羊畫一個口罩……我對我的花有責任！」

我把我畫的圖從口袋裡拿出來，小王子看到了，笑著說：「你的猢猻麵包樹看起來好像包心菜。」

「啊！」我原本還對我的猢猻麵包樹感到很得意呢！

「你的狐狸……他的耳朵……長得有點像角……而且太長了。」他又笑了起來。

「你這樣說我是不公平的，小王子。」我說：「除了畫過看得見大蟒蛇的內部和外觀的圖外，我不會畫別的東西。」我說。

「噢，那不要緊。」他說：「小孩子看得懂。」

於是，我用鉛筆畫了一副口罩，當我拿給他時，心裡很沉重。「你有一些我不知道的計畫……」

他沒有回答我，只說道：「你知道的，我來到地球……明天就是一周年了……」他沉默了一會後，繼續說道：「我降落的地方離這裡很近……」他臉紅了起來。

一股莫名的悲傷又湧上我的心頭，我起了一個疑問：「那麼，八天前，我遇見你的那天早上，你一個人在曠無人煙的沙漠上走，那並不是偶然的，而是你正要回到降落的地方囉？」

p. 146 小王子的臉又紅了。

我遲疑了一下説道：「會不會……是剛好滿一周年的緣故呀？」

小王子臉又紅了。他從不回答問題，不過當一個人臉紅，不就是在默認嗎？

「哦。」我對他説：「我有點擔心……」

他説道：「你現在得去工作了，回去修理引擎，我會在這裡等你，你明天晚上再回來。」

可是我不放心。我想起了那隻狐狸，一旦被馴服了，就會哭泣的。

26

p. 147 在水井旁，有一面殘缺的石牆。第二天晚上，當我工作完回來時，遠遠地我看到小王子坐在石牆上，兩腳懸空晃動著。我聽到他在説：「難道你忘了，這裡不是正確的地點。」想必有另外一個聲音回答了他，因為我聽到他又説道：「是的，沒錯！時間是對的，不過地點不對……」

我繼續朝石牆走去，仍然沒有看到或聽到其他什麼人的。但小王子繼續回答道：「當然了，你可以看到我的腳印是從哪裡開始的，你只要在那裡等我就對了。我今天晚上會在去那裡。」

我離石牆只有二十公尺遠，但我還是沒看到其他什麼人。

沉默了一會之後，小王子又説道：「你的毒液管用嗎？你確定它不會讓我痛苦太久嗎？」

我停了一下腳步，心砰砰跳，但仍不明白這是怎麼一回事。

p. 146–147 「現在走開吧。」小王子說：「我要從牆上下來了。」

我往牆腳下一看，嚇了一跳。那裡有一隻黃色的蛇，正面對著小王子，他的毒液可以讓人在三十秒內死亡。

我從口袋裡掏出手槍時，蛇聽到了我的腳步聲，於是他像一道細細的噴泉鑽進沙地裡。他不疾不徐地沒入石頭堆中，並微微發出了金屬般的聲音。

我抵達牆邊時，正好及時接住我的小朋友，他的臉色慘白如雪。

「這究竟是怎麼一回事？你在和一條蛇講話？」

p. 150–151 我把他一直戴著的金黃色圍巾鬆開，用水潤了潤他的太陽穴，讓他喝了些水。此時我什麼都不敢多問了，他面色凝重地看著我，兩手摟住我的脖子。我感覺到他的心跳猶如一隻被槍擊中的垂死小鳥的心跳一般。他對我說：「我很高興你找出了引擎的毛病出在哪裡了，現在你的飛機又可以飛了……」

「你是怎麼知道的？」我正是要來告訴他，我的飛機已經修理好了，這是我原先不敢奢望的。

他沒有回答我的問題，只說道：「我今天也要回家了……」他難過地繼續說：「那路途更遠……也更艱難。」

我清楚地瞭解到有什麼不尋常的事情發生了。我像抱著嬰兒一般地把他抱在懷裡，但他彷彿逕自落向一個深淵裡，我無法阻止他。

他表情凝重，遙望著遠方。「我有你給我的綿羊。我有綿羊的箱子。我還有口罩……」他露出傷感的笑容。

許久之後，他精神稍微好了些。「小傢伙，你剛剛在害怕……」他在害怕，這是無庸置疑的。

他微微笑了笑。「今天晚上我應該會更害怕……」

我再度感受到一種無法挽回的感覺，我心頭一顫。我知道，我無法忍受再也聽不到他的笑聲。對我來說，這笑聲就如沙漠中的一脈清泉。

p. 152–153 「小傢伙，我想再聽聽你的笑聲……」

但他說：「今晚，就要一年了，我的星星剛好會在我降落的地方的上空……」

「小傢伙，告訴我，你和蛇講的話，什麼會面的地方，什麼星星的，都只是一場惡夢，對不對？……」

他沒有回答，只說：「重要的事情是肉眼看不見的……」

「是的，我知道……」

「就像那朵花一樣。如果你愛某顆星星上面的一朵花，那在夜晚仰望星空就是一件很甜美的事，所有的星星都會綻放出花朵……」

「是啊，我知道……」

「也和那水一樣。你給我喝的水就像音樂一樣，因為那轆轤、繩索……你記得嗎……那水很甘甜的。」

「我當然記得……」

「在夜晚，你仰望星空。我住的星球太小了，我無法指出它在哪裡。這樣也好，你會覺得我的星球就在那些星星當中，所以所有的星星你都會喜歡看，它們都會成為你的朋友。另外，我還要送你一份禮物。」他又笑了起來。

「啊，小王子，小王子呀，我喜歡聽到你這個笑聲！」

「那就是我的禮物，……就好像那水一樣……」

「你說的是什麼？」

他回答：「人們眼裡的星星並非都一樣，對旅人來說，它們是嚮導；對另一些人來說，星星只是一些小光點；又如對學者來說，星星是要探討的問題；對我那位商人朋友來說，星星是財富。但所有的星星，都緘默不語。對你來說，在你眼裡的星星，將和其他人的星星都不一樣。」

p. 154–155 「你是指？」

「我就住在這些星星當中的其中一顆，我會在那上面笑著，因此當你仰望星空時，就好像所有的星星都在笑著。在你眼裡，星星是會笑的！」

説罷，他又笑了起來。

「還有，當你得到慰藉時（時間最終會撫平所有的哀傷），你會很高興認識了我，我們會永遠都是朋友，你會想要和我一起歡笑。因此，有時候你會打開窗戶，只是因為想快樂一下……當你的朋友們看到你對著天空大笑時，他們會感到訝異不解，那時，你就會對他們説：『沒錯，星星常會令我大笑！』而他們則會認為你瘋了。這將會是我跟你開的一個大玩笑……」

他又笑了。

「那就好像我給你的不是星星，而是許多會笑的小鈴鐺……」

他又笑了起來，然後又一臉認真地説：「今天晚上……你知道的……不要來。」

「我不離開你。」我説。

「我會看起來好像很痛苦、像快要死掉的樣子，大概就這麼一回事，你就別來看了，沒有必要的。」

「我不離開你。」

他焦慮了起來。「我告訴你……因為那條蛇也會在，你絕對不能被牠咬到，牠們有時候很壞的，會咬咬人來找樂子……」

「我不離開你。」

這時，他有點放心地説：「也對，牠們咬第二口的時候就沒有多餘的毒液了……」

p. 154–155 當天晚上，我沒有看到他動身，他不聲不響地離開了。當我終於趕上他時，他正快步走著，毫不遲疑。他只對我說了一句：「啊！你來了。」他牽著我的手，心裡頭還是很擔憂。「你不應該來的，你會很難受的，因為我看起來會像死掉的樣子，不過那不是真的……」

我沒說話。

「你知道的，路太遠了，我沒辦法帶著這個身體一起走，它太重了。」

我仍然沒說話。

「不過它會像一個蛻去的殼一樣，沒有什麼好令人難過的……」

我還是沒說話。

他有些氣餒，但又振作起來地說：「你知道，這會是很美好的。我也會仰望著星星，所有的星星上面都會有生了銹的轆轤水井，都會倒出水給我喝……」

p. 158–159 我仍舊一語不發。

「那真有趣啊！你會有五億個小鈴鐺，我會有五億個清新的泉水……」接著，他也不再作聲，因為他哭了……

「就是這裡。讓我自己一個人過去吧。」

他坐了下來，心裡在害怕著。然後他又說道：「你知道的……我的花……我必須對她負責。她是那麼的嬌弱！那麼的天真！她僅有四根一點也派不上用場的刺，來保護她抵禦這個世界……」

我也坐了下來，因為我再也站不住了。

他說：「好了……就這樣了……」

他遲疑一會兒後站了起來。他邁開了一步，我卻無法動彈。

在他的腳踝附近有一道黃色的光閃了一下。有一刻，他一動也不動，也沒有發出聲音，然後他像一棵樹般地緩緩倒下。因為是在沙地上的緣故，一點聲響也沒有。

27

p. 160–161 迄今已經六年過去了……我從未向人說過這個故事。迎接我歸來的朋友都很高興見到我仍活著。但我很悲傷，不過我告訴他們說：「太累的緣故。」

如今，我的悲傷已經得到一些紓緩。也就是說……不是完全消失。但是我知道，他確實已經回到他的星球了，因為在天亮的時候，我找不到他的身體。他的身體沒那麼重……夜晚時，我喜歡傾聽星星的聲音，那就像五億個小鈴鐺……

可是有一件很特別的事情……當我幫小王子畫口罩的時候，忘了畫皮帶上去，所以他是無法把羊套上口罩的。

因此，我就想：「他的星球現在怎樣了？或許，羊已經把花給吃了……」

有時我會對自己說：「一定不會的！小王子每天晚上都會把花放在玻璃罩裡，而且他非常小心地看守著他的綿羊……」這時，我就會覺得很快樂，所有的星星也都笑得很甜美。

可是，有時我又會對自己說：「人難免都會有疏忽的時候，而一次也就夠了！要是某個晚上他忘了把花放進玻璃罩內，或是綿羊在夜裡不聲不響地偷跑出來……」這時，這些小鈴鐺就變成了一顆顆的淚珠！

p. 163 對也喜愛小王子的你而言，這是很奧妙的。對我來說，在一個無人知道的某個地方，一隻我們沒見過的羊，不管牠有沒有把一朵玫瑰花給啃掉，整個宇宙都會變得不一樣了……

仰望天空，問問你自己：「羊究竟有沒有把花給吃了啊？」

然後，你就會看到整個世界都變了……

大人們永遠都不會明白這個問題是多麼的重要！

p. 164 對我來說，這裡是世上最美麗又最淒涼的地方。它和前一頁畫的是同一個地方，但我又把它再畫了一次，好讓你們看得更清楚。這裡，就是小王子降落地球並且消失的地方了。

仔細看看這幅圖畫，好讓哪天你到非洲去旅行時，可以辨認出來這個地方。如果你恰巧經過這個地方，請不要匆匆而過，在這顆星星的下方等一會兒吧！如果這時走來了一個小孩，他笑著臉，一頭金髮，而且不回答問題，那你就知道他是誰了。要是你遇到了，請你幫個忙，不要讓我再繼續難過下去了：請趕快寫封信告訴我，他又回來了……

Answers

P. 182 **A** ❶ innocent ❷ pity ❸ engine
❹ occupation ❺ outside ❻ sunsets

B ❶ The little prince's flower thought she was the only rose in the universe. (T)
❷ The fox was tamed by the little prince. (T)
❸ Most grown-ups understood the author's drawings. (F)
❹ The rose was the most precious thing on the little prince's planet. (T)
❺ The author forgot to draw a crate for the sheep. (F)
❻ The rose was very vain. (T)

P. 183 **C** ❶ Why was the businessman counting the stars? (b)
❷ When the author drew the muzzle for the sheep, what did he forget to do? (c)

D ❶ The little prince met a lamplighter on a very small planet.
❷ The little prince went back to his own star.
❸ A fox told the little prince a secret.
❹ The little prince found a garden of roses.
❺ The geographer asked the little prince about his home planet.

❶ → ❺ → ❹ → ❸ → ❷

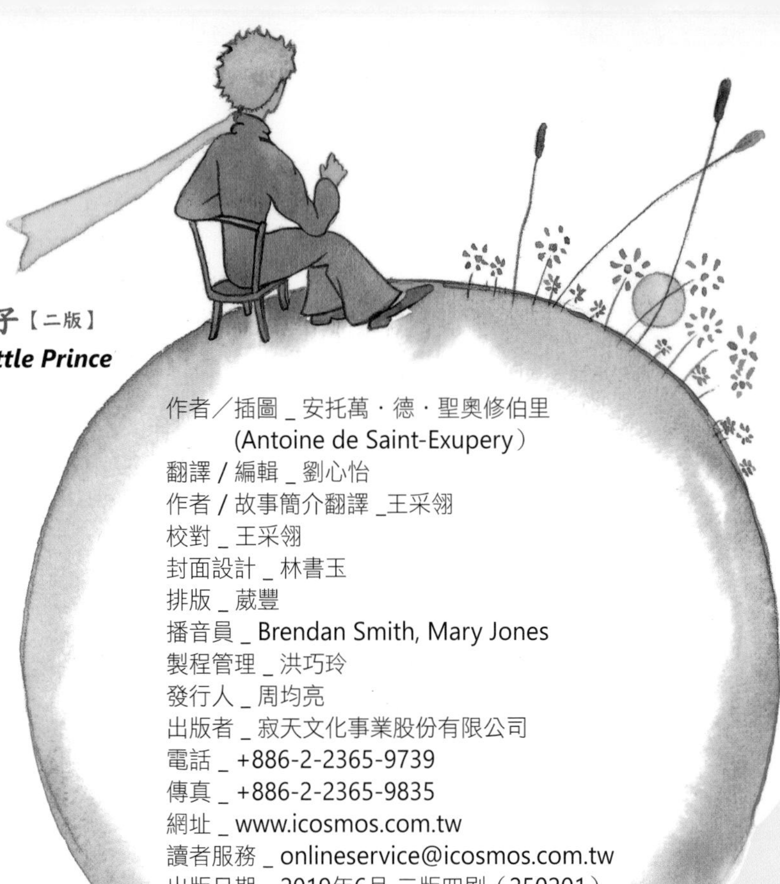

小王子【二版】

The Little Prince

作者／插圖 _ 安托萬．德．聖奧修伯里
(Antoine de Saint-Exupery）
翻譯 / 編輯 _ 劉心怡
作者 / 故事簡介翻譯 _王采翎
校對 _ 王采翎
封面設計 _ 林書玉
排版 _ 葳豐
播音員 _ Brendan Smith, Mary Jones
製程管理 _ 洪巧玲
發行人 _ 周均亮
出版者 _ 寂天文化事業股份有限公司
電話 _ +886-2-2365-9739
傳真 _ +886-2-2365-9835
網址 _ www.icosmos.com.tw
讀者服務 _ onlineservice@icosmos.com.tw
出版日期 _ 2019年6月 二版四刷（250201）
郵撥帳號 _ 1998620-0 寂天文化事業股份有限公司

國家圖書館出版品預行編目資料

小王子 / Antoine de Saint-Exupery 著 . -- 二版 .
-- [臺北市] : 寂天文化 , 2019.06 印刷
面；　公分 . -- (Grade 4 經典文學讀本)

ISBN 978-986-318-809-4(25K 平裝附光碟片)

1. 英語 2. 讀本

805.18　　108008057